D0424256

EYES OF THE *RIGEL*

Also by Roy Jacobsen in English translation

The Burnt-out Town of Miracles
Child Wonder
Borders

THE INGRID BARRØY TRILOGY
The Unseen
White Shadow
Eyes of the Rigel

ROY JACOBSEN

EYES OF THE *RIGEL*

Translated from the Norwegian by
Don Bartlett and Don Shaw

BIBLIOASIS
Windsor, Ontario

EYES OF THE *RIGEL*

ROY JACOBSEN

EYES OF THE *RIGEL*

Translated from the Norwegian by
Don Bartlett and Don Shaw

BIBLIOASIS
Windsor, Ontario

Copyright © Cappelen Damm AS
English translation copyright © 2020
by Don Bartlett & Don Shaw

First published in the Norwegian language as *Rigels Øyne*
by Cappelen Damm AS, Oslo, in 2017

First published in Great Britain in 2020
by MacLehose Press, London
an imprint of Quercus Editions Ltd
An Hachette UK Company

First published in North America in 2022
by Biblioasis, Windsor, Ontario

This translation has been published with the financial support of NORLA

All rights reserved. No part of this publication may be reproduced or transmitted in any
form or by any means, electronic or mechanical, including photocopying, recording, or any
information storage and retrieval system, without permission in writing from the
publisher or a licence from The Canadian Copyright Licensing Agency (Access
Copyright). For an Access Copyright licence, visit www.accesscopyright.ca or call toll free
to 1-800-893-5777.

FIRST EDITION
2 4 6 8 10 9 7 5 3 1

Library and Archives Canada Cataloguing in Publication

Title: Eyes of the Rigel / Roy Jacobsen ; translated from the Norwegian by Don Bartlett
and Don Shaw.
Other titles: Rigels øyne. English
Names: Jacobsen, Roy, 1954- author. | Bartlett, Don, translator. | Shaw, Donald, translator.
Series: Biblioasis international translation series ; 37.
Description: Series statement: Biblioasis international translation series ; 37 | Translation of:
Rigels øyne. | Previously published: London: MacLehose Press, 2021.
Identifiers: Canadiana (print) 20220132836 | Canadiana (ebook) 20220132860
ISBN 9781771964753 (softcover) | ISBN 9781771964760 (ebook)
Classification: LCC PT8951.2.A3854 R5413 2022 | DDC 839.823/74—dc23

Readied for the press by Daniel Wells
Cover illustration by Joe McLaren
Designed and typeset by Libanus Press in Adobe Caslon

PRINTED AND BOUND IN CANADA

PROLOGUE

From the sky, Barrøy resembles a footprint in the sea, with some mutilated toes pointing west. Except that no-one has ever seen Barrøy from the sky, other than the bomber crews, who did not know what they were seeing, and the Lord God, who does not appear to have had any purpose with this imprint He has left in the sea.

Snow is now falling heavily on the island, making it white and round – this lasts for one day and a night. Then its inhabitants will begin to form a black grid of tracks criss-crossing the whiteness, the widest of them will connect the two farmhouses, the old, run-down building on the island's highest point, surrounded by a cluster of trees, and the new one in Karvika, which is resplendent and showy, and in the summer is reminiscent of a stranded ark.

Then paths will appear between the farmhouses and the barn and the wharf buildings and boathouse and peat-stacks and potato cellars and haylofts and moorings, between the islanders' workplaces and stores, paths that will become entwined into a tangle of wild, random squiggles, the marks of children and play and ephemerae; there are many youngsters on the island in this, the first year of peace, there have never been more.

And then a dirty-brown rivulet winds its way south-west through the landscape, it is the sheep going to graze on the seaweed in the south of the island. Barbro hobbles along behind them, wielding a pitchfork and singing at the top of her voice, her face turned to meet the dancing snowflakes, which she snaps at between the strains of her song.

One might speculate about why she doesn't drive the animals down between the new wharf building and the Swedes' boat-house, the shortest distance between the barn and the sea. But Barbro knows what she is doing, it is late winter and the sea-weed is in the south, knotted together by storms and driving rain into brownish-black ropes, and left in coils at the highest point of the tide, where it lies, rank and covered in ice.

Barbro shuffles back and forth, pulling the strands apart so that the animals can get to the semi-frozen sustenance they contain, she is soon hot and sweaty and sits on the tree trunk they found drifting here a lifetime ago and secured with pegs and lines hoping that one day it would be worth something. And she begins to ask herself whether they have too many sheep this year, whether these undernourished creatures will manage to carry their lambs through to April and May, at this time of year she always frets about these things – every season has its worries, even the summer, when it can rain for months on end.

But then she feels a stinging sensation behind her left ear, it extends down the back of her neck, into her shoulder, along the arm that is resting on the tree trunk and into her hand. A hot, inner stream flows from Barbro's head and starts to drip from her longest finger, which immediately stiffens and creaks, as if made of glass.

She opens her eyes and realises that she is lying on her back, the snowflakes are falling on her eyes, she blinks and sees that Lea, the sheep, is standing at her side, staring out to sea, now whiter than ever, it is as calm as milk, there are no birds, except for the three cormorants sitting on the skerry to which they have given their name, and not even they are making any sound.

Barbro digs her fingers into Lea's wet fleece and drags herself to her feet. The other sheep stand watching. She picks up the pitchfork, feels a protracted stab of pain pass through her waist, and herds the flock in front of her up the same track, to the marsh pond where they cut peat in the summer. She knocks a hole in the ice crust so that the animals can drink, and one by one they waddle up the slope unprompted and disappear into the barn.

Finally Barbro sets off, her right hand still buried in Lea's wool, and she doesn't let go until this sheep, too, is swallowed up by the darkness. She bolts the door behind her and stands with her gaze fixed on the farmhouse, but fails to see the hand waving in the kitchen window. Barbro turns and follows the path leading to the new wharf house, goes into the baiting shed and stares down at the three holes in the bottom of an empty line-tub as the wind rattles a loose board in the south-facing wall. She sits down, grabs a bodkin and twine, and her hands set about making netting. The door opens and a voice asks what she is sitting here for.

"Aren't tha freezen?"

It is Ingrid, who had seen her aunt from the kitchen window and wondered why after going down to the quay, which Barbro often does, she hadn't come back up to the house today, and a long time had passed, evening was drawing in.

Barbro turns and fixes her with an intent gaze, and asks:

"Who ar tha?"

Ingrid moves closer and peers at her, tucks a few strands of hair under her headscarf and realises that she will have to answer this absurd question truthfully, and at great length.

1

It is summer on Barrøy, 1946, the down has been gathered, the eggs are in barrels, the fish have been collected from the racks and weighed and tied, the potatoes have been planted, the lambs are gambolling in the Acres, and the calves have been weaned from their mothers. The peat has to be cut, and the old house needs painting so it has no cause to feel ashamed beside the new one. From the hill behind the barn, Ingrid Barrøy is watching the boat in the bay, a cloud of terns above it, it is a whale catcher, the *Salthammer*, which they acquired when the previous owner went bankrupt, the Barrøyers have become whalers.

The *Salthammer* has a harpoon cannon on the bow and, on the mast, a white crow's nest with a black ring around its middle, it has rigging like a sailing ship and a wheel atop the wheelhouse roof, encircled by a white tarpaulin, there is a bait house and a modern line-setter, it is an imposing vessel for all seasons and occasions. Ingrid can hear the sound of hammering and sees Lars and Felix making preparations for the first whale hunt, small boys running to and fro along the deck, she can hear their voices rising and falling from across the water, and Kaja is sleeping on her back in a shawl.

Then her daughter wakes up. Ingrid unwraps her and lets her crawl about in the heather to her heart's content, and is startled at the sight of her jet-black eyes, takes her into her arms and walks down the hill towards the garden, where the soft-fruit bushes have begun to bud. She sits on the well-cover next to the newly purchased tub of paint and brushes, there are so many things that have to be done on the island, it has never had a brighter future, it has never had so many inhabitants, and it is no longer hers.

Ingrid goes into the kitchen and places Kaja on Barbro's lap, walks down to the shore and rows the færing out to the *Salthammer*, waits until Lars looks over the gunwale and asks whether she has brought him some coffee.

Ingrid says they have coffee on board, don't they.

Lars laughs and tells her they have managed to find a harpooner and will pick him up in Træna in a week, weather permitting.

Ingrid rests on the oars and says she will be rowing over to Adolf's in Malvika with the young'un, this evening, in the færing.

Lars asks what she wants to see Adolf about.

Ingrid shrugs, Lars says it's no skin off his nose, they've got enough boats.

To Ingrid this seems a rather high-handed attitude regarding the island's assets, so she says she is going to be away for a while.

"Ar tha now?"

The small boys come to the railing, too, Hans and Martin and, behind them, lanky Fredrik, who in the course of the winter has grown taller than is good for him. They spot Ingrid, immediately lose interest, and pester Lars to be allowed to shoot the harpoon, they can practise on some old fish crates they have seen on the shore, can't they.

Lars laughs and lifts up three-year-old Oskar so that he too can look down at Ingrid, who waves to him. Then Felix also appears, clutching some cotton waste between his oil-blackened fingers – such that all Barrøy's men, both big and small, are standing in line on the deck of the island's economic future, like an unsuspecting farewell committee, as Ingrid Marie Barrøy lays into the oars and rows back ashore, relieved that this has been much easier than she had feared.

She walks up to the house and also tells Barbro and Suzanne that she is going away for a while, casually dropping the news as if it were an everyday matter. But here in this women's world it turns into something rather more serious than it ought to be. Barbro has questions about where she is planning to go, why, and for how long? While Suzanne understands what is afoot and remarks contemptuously that Ingrid is lucky to have someone to miss, to search for, then hurries out to hang the washing on the drying rack.

Ingrid packs the small suitcase she takes with her whenever she tries to leave the island. And after she has gone down to the shore and wrapped Kaja up inside the canvas bag and settled her on the sheepskins at the back of the færing, before putting the suitcase in the forepeak, there is only Barbro, now transformed, who has a sense of the gravity of the situation, she stands and says goodbye with her arms crossed, her dress is sky blue, newly acquired with the proceeds of the winter, it is covered with huge white flowers, she says:

"We war goen t' paint th' hus, warn't we?"

"A'm not stoppen thas."

Barbro fidgets uneasily and says it's not possible to paint a house without Ingrid. Ingrid laughs and says they can wait until she gets back then.

"Reit," Barbro says. "An' hvan will tha bi comen bak than?"

"It'll bi some taim."

"Some taim," Barbro repeats, standing on the shore, in such a huff, as Ingrid manoeuvres the boat around Nordnæset, that she can't bring herself to wave until it is too late. By then the sun is in the north, low and white, and beneath it lies the sea, like a grey stone floor.

2

Kaja slept the whole crossing. When, at the break of dawn, Ingrid had cast the grapnel in Malvika bay on the main island, she curled up on the same sheepskins, the cries of seagulls, the gurgling sea and the gentle cooing of the eider ducks in her ears, and her eyes salty with sleeplessness. She fell asleep and woke up, and was dizzy and cold when she at last caught the smell of birch wood and saw a window opening in the white-walled farmhouse, and two eiderdowns being thrust out into the morning air.

The porch door opened, Daniel emerged with his braces dangling around his thighs, a saw in his hand and a coil of rope over his shoulder, and sauntered off in the direction of the forest. Then two girls came out, Liljan, Ingrid presumed, Daniel's younger sister, the other might well have been his sweetheart ... And now the pressure on her was so overpowering that she felt she had no choice but to row home again empty-handed, to give up on this endeavour before it ended in disaster.

But they had seen her.

Daniel re-emerged from the forest, leading a horse. He let go of the reins and strolled slowly down towards the harbour where he stood until Ingrid had manoeuvred the boat so close that it wasn't necessary to shout.

"Is that tha, Ingrid?"

She threw the mooring ropes ashore, and he dragged the færing in onto the skids. "And the baby," he said with a surprised smile.

Ingrid was unable to explain to him why she was there, but could at least get to her feet and pick up her sleeping daughter and wait for Daniel to notice the suitcase and carefully lift it onto land. Then she followed, mumbling that she would like to have a few words with Adolf, how was he doing?

Daniel said that his father had got old, and asked:

"Ar tha goen travellen?"

By this time the two girls had also come down to the shore. Ingrid showed them Kaja, who woke up and blinked. She shook Liljan's hand and introduced herself, they didn't know each other, there was a sea between them, and Malvika folk were farmers. A sumptuous farmhouse with three dormer windows stood in all its majesty on the hillside, encircled by two enormous trees, barns, cowsheds and summer livestock shelters, sheds, dairy cows and a host of goats and sheep, potatoes for sale, carrot fields, chickens, pigs, in addition to no fewer than six tenant farmers in various houses and timber cabins to the south along the coast. Even though Adolf in his younger days had been both a much-feared skipper of a cargo boat and a fish wholesaler, after losing two of his brothers when their boat sank, he had turned his back on the sea and transformed the family farm into an estate.

They laughed at the way Liljan held Kaja, who just smiled, and the girl who was new to Ingrid was allowed to hold her too, she was the daughter of one of the tenant farmers and worked as a maid in the main farmhouse, Ingrid was told, her name was Malin. They were commenting on the child's pretty nose and dark eyes when Ingrid noticed the door of the farmhouse opening again, and the old man himself, Adolf, emerged in a white shirt and with a skipper's cap on his head, he was dragging a kitchen chair, which he placed in the grass next to a rockery. He sat down and pulled out a pipe and carefully filled it, waiting for the guest to be done with the young ones and tell him the purpose of her visit, nobody rows over from the islands without any purpose, usually it is something important, too.

All the peace after the war had made Adolf hunched and stooped, and ruddier than Ingrid remembered. But he had those same darting eyes, which made everyone he talked to wonder whether he was about to end the conversation. Now Ingrid stood in front of him, with her immense lack of anything sensible to say, and an infant in her arms, which, it seemed, was more or less what Adolf had been expecting. The young people left, and he asked if she war starven.

Ingrid ignored the question.

They hesitated, her standing, him sitting, until Adolf raised his eyes and stared almost directly at her before remarking that she had no doubt come to ask him about the letter he had returned to her about a year ago, the letter she had given the Russian P.O.W. from the *Rigel*?

Ingrid said yes, why had Adolf taken the letter from Alexander, it had been meant to help him on his escape route home?

Adolf said it was a terrible note, she had also written her full name on it, as well as her address, Barrøy, when there was a war going on.

Ingrid nodded, and asked what he had done with Alexander.

Adolf said that question had been a long time coming.

Ingrid nodded again.

Adolf said that he had known her father, and her mother, they were good folk, but her mother had had a problem with her nerves, hadn't she?

Ingrid could only nod to that, too.

Her silence seemed to weary Adolf, who told her they had hidden the Russian in the loft for a little over a week, only Mathea had known about him, she had given him food and tended to his hands, and his wounds did heal, although his fingers would never be the same again.

Then one night when there was a snowstorm they had furnished him with a map and compass and sent him over the mountains to the harbour in Innøyr, where one of Adolf's old friends had taken him on board a freighter named the *Munkefjord*, it was from Finnmark and transported iron, it still did, he had shares in that boat.

And since Ingrid had nothing to add on this occasion either, he laughed in her face and said that by now she *must* be proper starven, they should go inside to see our Mathea, she's laikly bin watchen us from th' window an' put th' coffee on.

Mathea had been a housekeeper on the farm since long before the children's mother died, and ruled the roost in a sand-scoured kitchen gleaming with newly burnished copper and gloss paint, smelling of coffee and carbolic soap, where even the brass bar on the stove shone and the wood scuttle looked as if it were an exhibition piece. She was almost as old as Adolf, small, nimble and bow-legged, with hard, dry hands and a blue-checked headscarf bound so tightly that it resembled a helmet.

She averted her eyes as soon as Ingrid greeted her, and a look was exchanged between her and Adolf. Ingrid was asked to take a seat.

"O'er thar, next t' th' window," Mathea commanded before taking up a position at the head of the table, as if to conduct an inspection of Kaja. And it was thorough, she stroked the tiny chin with her crooked finger, making Kaja smile, exchanged a few more glances with Adolf and said – as though Ingrid were not present – Ya, that's 'im.

19

Adolf heaved a sigh in the direction of the tablecloth and mumbled that he hadn't paid such close attention out there in the sunshine, he didn't trust his eyesight any longer, but if Mathea was sure, then so was he, Ingrid could bet her life on it.

Ingrid asked whether folk gossiped about her in the village.

"Jus let 'em gossep," Adolf said, sticking a sugar lump in his mouth.

"Ya, the' need someth'n t' blather about," Mathea said, as if it weren't only Ingrid they discussed, the country had just emerged from a war, and wars do strange things to people, and not necessarily to their advantage.

Ingrid looked at her enquiringly.

Adolf said that folk knew about the child, but not about the father, not even Daniel knew about the Russian.

"An' does th' skipper on th' ship know?" Ingrid said. "Th' *Munkefjord . . . ?*"

Adolf said calmly that it all depended on what the Russian had told him. But now Ingrid should get some bread and butter down her and help herself to the lamb roast. And Mathea said, as though she had become aware of Kaja again:

"Sich a pretty babby."

Adolf said:

"Ya, ya . . ."

Mathea asked if she war still given titty.

Ingrid collected herself and managed to explain that she had lost her milk in the spring, and answered yes to Mathea's offer to warm some for her. She gave Kaja a piece of bread to suck, took off the child's headscarf and ran a finger along her tiny teeth. Before the milk arrived on the table Ingrid had also taken off Kaja's jacket, and heard Adolf's question as to what she was actually after, it was time to get to the point, wasn't it, clearly some sort of disquiet had been building up in him.

Ingrid asked if he knew where Alexander had left the ship.

"In Kongsmoen," Adolf said.

"Why Kongsmoen," Ingrid asked.

"Short distance to Sweden," Adolf said, and added that a road had been blasted up into the mountains, for a cableway to a mining community by the name of Skorovas, it was to transport untold amounts of pyrite from there, these were new times, the country was at peace, it had its own future back.

Ingrid asked if he thought Alexander had followed the "road" inland towards Sweden.

Adolf said there was no way of knowing, but that had been the plan, yes. And Ingrid began to suspect he was cooking up some kind of white lie.

She asked him to tell her everything he knew.

Adolf, who had a lifetime's experience of expressing himself in circuitous terms, said that Ingrid was making a great mistake if she was now sitting at his table and planning to follow the fellow, to undertake anything like that would be madness.

But he said this without looking at her, and seemed more relieved than resigned when Ingrid said nothing in a manner that could be interpreted in no other way than that she had already made up her mind, or else that she was doing so at this very moment, and that from now on there was no turning back.

Mathea broke this pregnant silence and said she had been the housekeeper on Adolf's farm since she was a young girl, for fifty-nine years, she totted up, and that is a lot of time, so Ingrid should think things through very carefully before she did anything stupid.

Ingrid said she had been thinking about it all winter, and with the light in the spring and summer improving, things could not be any worse now than they had been.

Mathea stared at her, and Ingrid stared back. Mathea said love is treacherous. Yes, Ingrid said.

They talked about peace-time and the radical changes to Barrøy since Daniel had been there last autumn doing a sterling job of restoring the island after it had been neglected for so long, those little miracles that allow an island to flourish again after a disaster, the fish, the people, the land and the animals, Adolf wanted to know every detail, including about the lightning that had struck Barbro, this woman who had always been a beacon in the seas around her.

Ingrid said that Barbro had recovered from the stroke, her aunt had learned to speak again, and knew who she was, she also knew who the others were, all of them, but she didn't want to go out in a boat anymore, she had become afraid of the sea.

Adolf said that Our Lord also has a purpose with whatever He taketh away – what on Earth might seem confusing and meaningless can make good sense in Heaven.

To Ingrid this sounded both hollow and long-winded, but she agreed that Barbro had been a beacon that was no longer there, that too was one of the reasons why she, Ingrid, now found herself here on the threshold of this journey – the stroke that incapacitated Barbro was the irrefutable sign that life is short and fragile. But she didn't say so aloud. And she didn't divulge the most important reason either: the fact that the older Kaja got, the blacker her eyes became and the clearer her gaze.

After both mother and child had been installed with inordinate care in the finest room of the house, which was always unoccupied, according to Mathea, such was Adolf's wealth, Ingrid sat on the wide bed searching through the window for Barrøy, as months ago Alexander must have sat here with this same view. But back then it was a winter's night, and now it was summer with all its light, and there was a knock at the door.

Ingrid was not accustomed to people knocking on her door, but there was another knock, so she said, yes, and Mathea came in, noticed that Kaja was asleep in the cradle under the window and sat down on the bed next to Ingrid. But she had just as little to say about the reason for her visit as Ingrid had had about hers. They remained where they were nonetheless, and it occurred to Ingrid that the old woman must have let an opportunity slip at some time in her life, without realising it, and was now sitting here reflecting deeply on it. Mathea sighed, rose to her feet and said, no, she couldn't stay here like this, wished Ingrid goodnight, and went out again, closing the door noiselessly behind her.

3

Next morning after breakfast Ingrid set about tackling the pass through the mountains that led to the landward side of the main island, rough, hard-going terrain, which was covered in snow all winter and melted so late in spring that it was a sign of approaching summer to the island folk when this did finally happen, but where now small ferns would tickle a wanderer's calves, and recognising an unmistakable footprint Ingrid felt a sensation shoot up from the soles of her feet into the clouds above, her head was reeling.

She wasn't walking alone, as Alexander had done, but was accompanied by Daniel and Liljan, and young Malin. Even Adolf and Mathea struggled up the twisting, overgrown cart track, still silently advising her against embarking on this search for a needle in a haystack. But Mathea was now less adamant and more pensive, and when they eventually shook hands at the highest point Ingrid felt confident of her quest. She had some provisions in a canvas bag that Daniel had tied to her suitcase, which he had fitted with leather straps so that she could carry it on her back. Kaja was asleep in a shawl tied around Ingrid's belly, and Ingrid didn't look back once the descent towards Innøyr had begun.

She drank water from every stream she crossed, and they stopped twice to eat before arriving at a new sea, and slept in a fisherman's shack, which one of Adolf's friends had unlocked for them, for two nights. Then they boarded a fishing boat, tendering a note from Adolf, which had the desired effect on the skipper, a small, thickset, taciturn man, who nodded impassively to his passengers and gave Ingrid his cabin, he could sleep in the chart house, he said, that was where he belonged. But he couldn't take them any further south than Rørvik, there Ingrid would have to wait for a another lift up the fjord to Kongsmoen, it's a long one, that fjord, he said, it almost cuts the country in two.

Yes, that's the plan, thought Ingrid, who was now on her way, and stood on the deck surveying familiar groups of mountains and islands, which, one by one, sank beneath the horizon behind her, leaving her without even the slightest trace of melancholy. Kaja, too, gazed at everything with stoic calm in her Russian eyes, this world they were in the process of leaving, which had been the only one they knew.

After three nights in Rørvik, which they spent in another shack, and where Ingrid whiled away the days alongside the quays with Kaja on her back or belly, the *Munkefjord* docked, fully loaded with masts for the cableway, sticking out all over the place, causing the ship to look like a floating magpie's nest. Ingrid went on board with yet another note from Adolf and addressed a great hairless lump of a man from Finnmark who went by the name of Emil Rimala, and Emil Rimala said:

"Ah, Adolf, old Adolf," and read the note twice, very carefully, before folding it up and handing it back, deep in thought, as if Ingrid hadn't made full use of it yet.

Ingrid asked whether there was anything wrong.

"No," Rimala said.

But when he was shown Kaja's eyes he was far less convinced than Mathea and Adolf had been. Nor did he exhibit any visible reaction when Ingrid told him that she wanted to be put ashore at the same place as the Russian.

"The Russian?"

"Yes."

"The one who'd been on the *Rigel*?"

"Yes."

"O.K.," Rimala said in American English, and Ingrid, who in the last few days had exchanged no more than a few banalities with a man at the harbour office in Rørvik, asked Rimala what he thought about her venture, as if she had begun to lose faith in it, or as if to elicit what Rimala had to say, there was something in that closed face of his that troubled her.

Rimala said that it was nothing to do with him.

Ingrid asked him what he remembered of the trip the previous winter, of the meeting with her Russian.

"Your Russian?"

"Ya, my Alexander."

Rimala said it wasn't the first time he had taken refugees on board, he had been involved in evacuating a whole population from Finnmark, his own people, it had been dark and miserable that winter, and who can remember one face from so many anyway? But yes, he did remember the Russian, unless that was just something he had pretended to be, because when he went ashore in Kongsmoen he had thanked Rimala with a stream of incomprehensible words, but he hadn't shaken his hand, he had held his hands up in the air by way of apology, they looked like feet.

"Ya," Ingrid said, "That's 'im."

But why would he pretend to be a Russian, if he wasn't one?

"Maybe because he was German," Rimala said. "A deserter."

Ingrid asked whether he would have taken a deserter on board?

"Yes," Rimala said, without hesitation. And again Ingrid showed him Kaja, who looked up in puzzlement at his shiny scalp. Rimala smiled back, avoiding her eyes, and Ingrid thanked him.

"For what?"

She said that helping Russian fugitives was a capital offence during the war, so he deserved a *big* thank-you. Rimala smiled with embarrassment, and said Ingrid had better have a word with Alf, his first mate, he was the one who had given the poor wretch something to eat, and he had also shared his cabin with him.

*

But Alf Isaksen wasn't the eyewitness she was seeking either, if anything he was just as dismissive as the skipper, and became even more annoyed when Ingrid wouldn't stop her pestering. But later that evening over the dinner table in the mess it transpired that Alf, too, remembered the Russian's hands. In addition, he had wondered at his high spirits, this evidently happy soul who was about to embark on an impossible trek over the mountains in mid-winter, it was 60 or 70 kilometres to the border alone and no doubt an eternity from there to the nearest sign of civilisation in Sweden, so why was he so happy?

To be alive, Ingrid suggested.

Alf Isaksen said that to make it alive through metre-deep snow from Kongsmoen to Sweden, you would need help from both God and your fellow man, otherwise it was certain death. And Ingrid reflected that to get help you would have to talk to someone, who would remember, such as Rimala and Alf, and not least herself, so she was grateful for his hands, which worked when Kaja's eyes did not.

She asked Alf why he was so bitter.

He looked at her in bewilderment and said he wasn't, he was just exasperated that she could even believe it was possible to track down a person who had disappeared during a war, it was like trying to comb the seabed. Ingrid had no further questions.

At around midnight she heard the skipper and his mate arguing loudly on the deck, they were going at it hammer and tongs. She realised they were talking about her, Rimala's Finnmark voice shouting above the roar of the engine that they had no choice, they had to let her go, while Alf, less voluble but no less intense, yelled that they were committing a grave sin, with respect to both the woman and God.

"To hell with you, and you can take God with you!"

"And the kid as well, a little baby! All because of that stupid booze ..."

The voices died down and the men left, but Ingrid couldn't sleep, she lay looking around the cabin that Alf had cleaned up for her while she stood watching, having been told not to help. He had also made up the only bunk. The smell of soap mingled with diesel, oil and the stale odour of men's sweat. On the outer bulkhead hung a notice headed with the word *Judenverbot*, daubed with many black crosses, together with a yellowing piece of paper describing how to connect car batteries in series. Between the notices gleamed a blue porthole, which Ingrid couldn't take her eyes off, until her heartbeat synchronised with the rhythm of the ship's engine.

4

The fjord lay like a grey belt between steep, green mountainsides, and early one morning the *Munkefjord* put in
at Kongsmoen in rain which came down in sheets, obscuring
forests, mountains and farmsteads, it was a dismal sight.

Ingrid had got herself ready, then dressed Kaja and strapped
her on her back. She went onto the deck carrying her suitcase
in her left hand and thanked both Rimala and Alf, who were
waiting for her by the rickety gangway, and stood for a moment
in front of them in case anything might occur to either man,
an explanation maybe of the racket she heard in the night, but
they just looked away shamefacedly and failed to utter a word
of farewell.

Ingrid walked off the ship and down a long, deserted pier in
the lashing rain and sought refuge in a general store situated
beneath an illegible, rusty sign at the end of an unpainted ware-
house. Absolutely drenched, she stepped just inside the door, on
which hung a small bell, and stared at the water streaming down
the dirty window-panes like warm gelatine, and felt a strange
rage deep inside her, as though the crew on the *Munkefjord*

had robbed her of something, and as though she – as a result – had become some weak, useless human being, even before the journey had really begun.

A throat cleared behind her. She moved to the side and let an elderly man out into the rain, heard the bell ring above the door and then a voice, from inside. She turned and saw a woman, a lot older than herself, a white smock covering a robust body, with flour on her sturdy hands and arms. Leaning over a scratched glass counter, she was rubbing her fingers together as if she were counting banknotes, and her two lustreless eyes were staring into space, showing not the slightest interest in the new arrivals. At least she straightened up.

Ingrid moved closer and explained the bizarre reason for her being in Kongsmoen, and there were a good deal of *eh's*? and *what's*? in two different dialects before Ingrid understood that the woman had no recollection of any refugees from the last year of the war, nor of any people who had been put ashore here to walk inland along the planned cableway route to the mines at Skorovas, and thence into Sweden. Neither did she believe that, even if there had been any, they would have taken *that* route, since the cableway was built by a firm named Bleichert and the mountains were crawling with Germans, so a refugee would probably have chosen the route along the fjord towards the coast, or south through Høylandet, wouldn't they . . . ?

"But those routes don't lead to Sweden, do they," Ingrid said.

"No," the woman said.

Ingrid put down her suitcase and sat on it and dried Kaja, who smiled, her eyelashes glistening with drops of rainwater. The woman appeared to have been given some food for thought, and came around the counter and said her name was Lilly, then placed a hand on Kaja's head, quickly withdrew it again, went back around the counter and disappeared through a door which swung shut many times behind her. All that could be heard was the rain.

Then she heard snatches of voices from the back room, angry shouts and nervous laughter. Lilly came out again, and said loudly that Ingrid was wet, the child, too – here's a towel, would she like some coffee?

Ingrid said yes, could she sit by the stove?

Lilly nodded, and remarked she'd had to light the fire this morning, what a miserable summer, and went to fetch a chair.

Ingrid sat down, and Lilly stood at her side.

Ingrid asked if there were any other places in the village where people could get food. Lilly understood that question, too, and gave her the name of the canteen at the mining works and a storeroom in one of the barracks, as well as the farms, of course, although she had never heard of any strangers stocking up there, and there was not much she didn't know about what went on in this place, she had served behind the counter here since she was a young girl.

"It was wartime," Ingrid said.

"Yes, and perhaps folk didn't say so much," Lilly admitted.

"Or rather," she corrected herself, "they probably said even more then, but not out loud."

They smiled at each other.

Ingrid asked if any dead bodies had been found in the mountains over the last few years.

Lilly said, well, there had been the occasional accident, she supposed, at the works, but no deaths, no, she'd not heard of any fatal cases.

She fetched two mugs of coffee and placed them on a tub of syrup and stood there as her lacklustre eyes filled with more and more life. She went to fetch another chair, then sat down beside Ingrid. No, Lilly had never heard of the *Rigel*, and had Ingrid really abandoned her house and home for the sake of this man, a person she could barely remember?

Ingrid retorted that she remembered him all too well.

"O.K., O.K.," Lilly said, and mumbled that she wanted to say that she hoped for the best, if that was of any use to her, but she did not dare.

Ingrid asked what that was supposed to mean. Lilly answered that she had hoped for so much in her life, but nothing had come of it. At that moment they looked each other in the eye, until Ingrid lowered her gaze, and discovered that her rage had gone.

Lilly asked how old she thought she was.

"*You?*"

"Yes."

"Hva does tha mean?"

"Hvur ald does tha think A am?" Lilly repeated, mimicking Ingrid's dialect. And Ingrid realised she must be teasing and said it was impossible to say. Lilly said it was nice of her to put it like that, stroked a floury hand back and forth over her right knee as though she had been given something uplifting to reflect on, as though she had begun to realise that this day was not going to be like all the others, and that all those other days, they had been far too long.

5

Ingrid sat by the stove as the customers came in to the tinkling of the bell and the squelching of various kinds of boots, mumbled brusque requests across the glass counter, received their goods and cast stolen glances at Ingrid and Kaja, who was crawling around on the floor. To the sound of teeming rain.

There was a smell of coal dust and flour, soured milk and liquorice, mixed with a touch of salted herring and camphor. Ingrid sat with Adolf's map on her knees. But she hadn't unfolded it. And a sketch pad, from her school days, to have something to take notes in, on the last four pages, which were blank, information which might come in useful, place-names and Alf Isaksen and Emil Rimala, the eyewitnesses who could hardly remember anything. She didn't look at the drawings from her time at school, they were behind her, though they still weighed on her mind.

An elderly man came up, doffed his cap and held it in his hand, he said he was the foreman at the cableway.

"A see," Ingrid said, then lifted up Kaja for him to inspect, no introduction was necessary here, Lilly had already seen to that.

He scrutinised the child, screwed up his eyes, and appeared to be pondering something, but shook his head and said he had never seen eyes like these. Nor had he heard anything even close to what he had just been told by Lilly over there, nor about the ship going down, nor about this Russian, nor the likes of what Ingrid was planning to do, as far as he had understood. But he would like to shake her hand, if she would allow him, and he also managed to perform what resembled a bow of condolence, and then he put his cap back on his head and disappeared into the rain.

Ingrid exchanged glances with Lilly, and Lilly shrugged.

At around noon Lilly brought some milk for Kaja, more coffee and a plate of waffles, as though she had resigned herself to the fact that her customers had come to stay. They ate, and Lilly asked if Ingrid had come to a decision yet.

"As t' hva?"

Lilly didn't answer.

Ingrid let her hold Kaja, since she looked as though she wanted to, and the window behind them was filled with a light that transformed the droplets of rain into sparkles, which were extinguished more slowly than the eye can register, until the glass was left just as dirty as before, all this water that does not wash, Ingrid reflected, a sentiment from the war which came back to her whenever she felt sullied. But then the door opened again and the foreman returned, stood in front of them and asked without any preamble whether Ingrid would be willing to sell him her suitcase.

"My suitcase?"

"Yes, it's made of leather, I can see. And those, they're brass fittings."

Ingrid said that it had belonged to her mother. It was the suitcase all the Barrøy women took with them when they left the island.

She couldn't cross the mountains with a suitcase, he said, she needed a rucksack, this one, and he would give her twenty kroner into the bargain.

Ingrid looked down at the rucksack he had placed at her feet, opened it and peered inside the empty pockets, it was made of grey sailcloth and had brown leather flaps, over the side-pockets too, and shoulder straps that could be adjusted to various lengths. She directed her gaze at Lilly, who had gone back behind the counter and shouted that the foreman should give Ingrid forty kroner.

"I haven't got that much," he said.

"Oh yes you have," Lilly snapped.

The foreman shook his head and left again. Soon afterwards the bell tinkled once more, he was back, and said:

"Thirty plus the rucksack?"

Ingrid's eyes wandered from the suitcase to the rucksack and up to the face of a person she would never understand – and said yes.

When he had left with the suitcase, Lilly offered to let her sleep in a room above the shop, then the following day her son could show Ingrid the way, he never went out, but now he had no choice, she would see to that. They themselves lived at the other end of the stockroom, there were only the two of them now, Lilly appreciated being able to walk from her bed to the shop and back without getting her feet wet.

Ingrid asked how old her son was.

Lilly was on the point of answering, but smiled instead, as if this were a joke, and asked whether Ingrid was trying to catch her out. Ingrid smiled back warily, and said that she didn't know what to do.

"Oh yes, you do," Lilly said. "You do know."

Then she said she would let Ingrid into a secret: she had been a widow for many years, but had found a new husband during the war. She had left him though.

Ingrid looked at her in puzzlement.

"He was useless," Lilly said.

"A see," Ingrid said.

"He wasn't from these parts," Lilly said. "He was German."

Ingrid nodded.

Lilly ran a hand across her face, leaving flour on her eye-lashes, and asked if she could hold Kaja again. Ingrid said yes. Lilly lifted Kaja up and looked as though she were crying and said that her nappy was heavy, didn't Ingrid change her?

Ingrid said nothing, she just stared.

Lilly laid Kaja on the glass counter and changed her, careful not to get any flour on the child's skin, and said that what she had just told Ingrid she hadn't told anyone else, and she never would, even though she suspected that the whole place already knew, and there is nothing small infants love more than a dry nappy.

She passed Kaja back – like a gift-wrapped present – and said this last year had been the hardest ever, a year she had hoped would be the best. Ingrid said she knew what she meant and told her about how she had found Alexander in the barn on Barrøy, like finding hidden treasure in the midst of a disaster, about the following days and nights that couldn't be expressed in words and would never be absent from her mind, and suddenly fell quiet. Lilly blinked, and mused for a moment, and said that maybe she could see some hope for Ingrid after all, even though this had now become even more difficult.

6

There are many ways of walking, and Ingrid Marie Barrøy was light of foot, in calf-length leather boots, with a rucksack on her back and Kaja on her belly, swaddled in the same shawl, which had now been reinforced with the straps Daniel had fastened around the suitcase that she no longer had, Barrøy's wonderful suitcase, which henceforth belonged to the foreman of the longest cableway in the country. Ingrid hadn't been given a name she could note down in her sketch pad, but Lilly's had been added. And ahead of her through the forest walked an overweight, breathless young man, who said not a word, Lilly's son, Carl.

After roughly a kilometre Ingrid had a feeling they were going in the wrong direction, and asked where he was taking her. Carl did no more than point up a gentle slope, covered with scrub, and nod, as though to convince himself, after which he plodded on in the same wrong direction. Accompanying them was a large, tar-brown dog, which walked at Ingrid's side, like a guard.

They found themselves between two hilltops, the forest became denser and the path narrower. Ingrid stopped again, and refused to go on, pointed at the sun and where the sea had to be, they could just make out the fjord through the foliage.

Over his shoulder, Carl said petulantly, what did *she* know about using the sun to find directions?

There was a nervous indecisiveness about him, as though he were looking intently for something he knew didn't exist. Whenever he stopped to catch his breath, he dug his fingers into the coat of the dog, which immediately sat on its haunches, so he could support himself on it, like a crutch.

In short panting breaths, he told Ingrid how hard a seaman's life was, he had been torpedoed twice, he told her about winter nights on an open raft, without food or fresh water, about dead comrades, he hadn't been in the forest since he came home, as it reminded him of the sea, the war had destroyed both, what did Ingrid think of the forest?

She looked around and her view had never been so restricted.

As a result she was unable to protest when once again he set off in the wrong direction and didn't stop until they were standing on the banks of a circular tarn that resembled an eye in the landscape, the leaves of the trees hanging over its banks like thick eyebrows, there was a smell of spruce needles, juniper and wet earth. They had come to an overgrown campsite, with a fireplace and the remains of a hut that looked as though it had been built by children. Carl said they should sit down, and Ingrid asked what they were doing here.

He said that they had to wait – for one of his friends.

Ingrid asked if it was Carl's voice she had heard from the back room in the general store yesterday, and he said yes, he usually sat there reading the magazines they sold. Then he said that Ingrid would never find her Russian again, because if it were true what his mother claimed, then he had survived a ship going down, and nobody does that.

Ingrid asked whether Carl had ever heard of the *Rigel*.

Carl said no, but one ship sinking is much like any other.

Ingrid asked if he had a job.

No.

Didn't he even help his mother in the shop?

If necessary, he might lift a few boxes and crates and roll in the odd barrel, yes.

And as Ingrid couldn't think of any other questions, she asked what the dog's name was.

He said it didn't have a name, and she should stop digging and delving.

Ingrid leaned forward so that Kaja could pat the dog, it licked her hands, and Kaja laughed. Something seemed to have occurred to Carl, he jumped up and began to scamper around the overgrown campsite, obviously found what he was looking for, and pulled a shoe box from a hole beneath a tree root, opened it and triumphantly held up a sheath knife, a whetstone and some fish-hooks, together with a short, thick candle. He had been given the knife by his grandfather, he said, and now finally he had found it again.

Ingrid noticed that it was a delicately crafted, expensive model, in a silver-mounted sheath. She asked whether that was why they were here, because of the knife.

"No," he said, they were here to wait, and to keep their mouths shut.

They waited until they heard noises in the forest. A figure appeared in the campsite, a lean, elderly man, who didn't look at Ingrid, but at once sat down on the log between them and, clearly disgruntled, muttered something to Carl.

Ingrid got to her feet and stood in front of them.

The newcomer, dressed in worn, blue dungarees and high-shafted, black boots, had the appearance of a farmer. A long, grey beard bobbed like a tie over his chest, and his sunken eyes didn't look at either of them as he reported that there had been a snowstorm in the mountains that night and Carl should not have asked him to come here, that was all he knew.

Neither Carl nor Ingrid said a word.

The dog sat down between the knees of the stranger. He patted it and, looking down at its shaggy coat, he said he had warned the Russian not to attempt the mountains after the ship's crew had hastily put him ashore, as they were afraid their contraband might be discovered, they were smuggling hard spirits. But the Russian had wanted to go nonetheless, at least he'd had something to eat.

"He *insisted* on going," he asserted, as if to defend a crime.

Ingrid asked Carl if his mother knew about this.

"No."

"An' hvur does *tha* know?"

Carl said that this man had given him the dog, he was a cargo surveyor at the harbour, an old friend of his father's. The cargo surveyor said that nobody could cross the mountains and survive, especially in a storm. And now he was going back down to the village.

Carl told him to tell Ingrid which way the Russian had gone.

"The cableway."

"Are you sure?"

"Yes."

He mumbled a few parting words down into the dog's coat, stood up and left. The reflection of a plane silently cut a diagonal across the tarn, it resembled an insect as it disappeared into the forest on the other side, at which point they also heard the sound, and Carl asked what Ingrid was going to do.

Ingrid said that she would carry on, she had no choice.

Carl nodded, put the other objects back in the box and shoved it under the tree root again, tucked the sheath knife under his belt and began to walk around the tarn, now with Ingrid's rucksack on his back.

She followed him up another mountainside and down into a wide valley. They crossed a marsh covered in white cotton grass swaying in an imperceptible wind and came to a road that wasn't a road to be used by people but rather a corridor hacked through the forest. Carl gave her the rucksack and pointed up the slope.

She thanked him. He said, as a kind of farewell, that no matter what she did or found, coming home again would be worse, nobody comes home. He looked at her one final time, turned and set off downhill.

The nameless dog continued up the slope with Ingrid until it heard a sharp whistle, stopped, looked at her, then was gone, hot on the heels of Carl, who seemed already to have sunk into the ground.

Ingrid sat down in the heather, and Kaja fell asleep. Ingrid lay beside her and did the same, falling into a slumber without the blue porthole of the *Munkefjord*, without the smell of diesel and sweat and the sound of men's angry voices on a rain-drenched iron deck. When she awoke, the cloud cover had lifted. The village of Kongsmoen lay beneath her, and a ship resembling the *Munkefjord* was towing a narrow, white fan along the unending fjord and out to sea.

7

On either side of the cableway path lay newly felled tree trunks, like enormous, knocked-out teeth, skirted by greyish-green columns of spruce which gave off small puffs of yellow pollen. Ingrid was walking in dry, sea-less heat, drinking from the streams that babbled through the silence, listening to the forest that sighed despite the lack of wind, and hearing the occasional bird, as she swatted midges and flies away from Kaja's face, and imagined what walking here in winter, in a storm, would be like. She was on the lookout for bodies or human remains, for something she on no account wanted to find, and she enjoyed the walking, as if every trace of evidence she failed to find brought her closer to her goal.

Here and there they came across groups of labourers dressed in black, with steam rising from their bodies, busy cementing foundations and raising iron masts, which they had dragged up using horses and tractors and their bare hands, men with portable forges and cement-mixing boards and spades and sledge-hammers, men of all ages from all corners of the country, who were provided with a welcome change at the sudden appearance of this woman in the middle of nowhere, and carrying a child on her belly, into the bargain.

They wiped the sweat from their brows, lit a cigarette, and cast their eyes over Kaja and shook their heads, and they had no memory of any Russian refugee. Not even those of them who had been here since Bleichert's time remembered any Russians. Nor had they found any remains, neither of animals nor humans. And the answer was always the same question: Why would a refugee have taken this route when it was swarming with Germans here at that time?

But they listened politely, and gave Ingrid some food and coffee, so she didn't need to eat any of Lilly's packed lunch, they flirted and laughed and chucked Kaja's chin, and took neither themselves nor Ingrid too seriously.

Ingrid walked on, but still didn't find what she had no wish to find, and saw neither birds of prey nor carrion crows. The next work gang she happened upon couldn't remember any Russians either, nor any other refugees for that matter, and they hadn't seen anyone, dead or alive, in the mountains. But they, too, were full of hope on Ingrid's behalf and cheerily sent her on her way, all sounding as though they meant it.

Ingrid and Kaja slept under a woollen blanket on a cold, insect-free night at the highest point, the new masts like a straight line of crucifixes stretching as far as the horizon behind them and nothing at all in the open wound ahead.

*

They spent the next night in some hay in a barn in Namdalen, and the following day were transported – by another kindly work gang who couldn't remember anything either – across a bottle-green river in an ore-bucket. From there they continued eastwards, past Angle Station 1 and into yet another valley, where the spruce trees stood like black palisades on either side of what was to be a horizontal paternoster performing a never-ending dance across the wide expanses, with six hundred kibble buckets hanging between 170 masts, up to a thousand metres apart, through a forest changing from spruce to fir, although Ingrid did not notice, and then to birch trees, which became shorter and shorter, eventually to be superseded by willow and juniper and heather, and this she did notice, because her view became wider and wider the higher she climbed – and she found nothing.

She travelled with the sun in her face, and then at an angle from the right, and finally beating down like a warming stove on her back, and arrived at the mining community of Skorovas late in the evening of the third day. Now they were over the mountains where snow still lay in an open landscape of rock and scrub. Ingrid was sweaty and stiff, but still light of foot, the journey had taken on its own momentum, it had become an autonomous, independent entity, she was searching for love, and was still happily unaware that truth is the first casualty of peace.

8

They were allowed to sleep on a mattress in the pantry of a semi-completed villa and were woken next morning by the sound of frenzied hammering. During the day Ingrid walked around talking to people in a town that was striving to raise itself from bare rock. She breathed in the smell of fresh, white timber, tar and paint and concrete, a town for six or seven hundred souls, with a school, a health centre, a post office, a chapel, a power station, maintenance and repair shops and stables and laundries and production units, a national dream that was in the process of coming true, it was dizzying, intoxicating and edifying, for the first time in her life Ingrid had a sense of witnessing prosperity, this is what prosperity looks like, this is what the future looks like, in a rich country.

But here, too, she was regarded as a surprising relic of a time that fortunately had gone, a person whose actions were almost completely devoid of any sense or reason – *a Russian*?

No, nobody had heard anything of the kind.

And here, too, people were friendly and willing to listen. Ingrid was told a whole host of perplexing, contradictory tales.

She was allowed to have a bath in a new wash-house and wash her clothes and nappies at the local shopkeeper's, a robust, talkative widower in his forties, whose name was Alfred Benjaminsen and who spoke the same dialect as herself, to such a degree that it was laughable, fancy meeting him *here*.

"Good t' see tha," he said, and seemed to regard both the *Rigel* and the missing Russian as a bad joke, so improbable was the story Ingrid was peddling.

They talked about mutual acquaintances they might have up on the northern coast, and they probably also visualised their respective home districts, Barrøy and an island a little further north, where Benjaminsen grew up. But the more concrete the details became, the more evasive he seemed to be and the vaguer his memory, until the conversation came to a complete halt, and Ingrid suspected that he, too, might have something to hide, just like Emil Rimala and Alf Isaksen on the *Munkefjord*.

She hadn't been in the town for more than a week when Benjaminsen, after closing time and a few too many, confided in her that Skorovas was actually his hiding place, or a new start in life, that he had to keep *a low profile*, even here, as he had sold fish to Germany during the war, and had become a wealthy man as a result, it was a heavy burden to bear, in peacetime.

Ingrid said that one of her acquaintances had sold fish to the Germans, too, a whaler.

Alfred Benjaminsen didn't bat an eyelid.

He drank more of the methylated spirit he kept on a hidden shelf beneath the counter. And he had rubbed something in his hair, which made it look like dry hay in the rain, a type of grease that he advertised on two posters outside the shop, next to tobacco, fishballs, matches, and corsets with stays for ladies who were too fat. There were many women in the town, he called them all ladies, and he became more and more indiscreet, a man who was suffering from some deep sorrow, as far as Ingrid could make out, who let his tongue run away with him, and snuffled, and eventually fell asleep on a wave-shaped sofa that filled almost the whole of the back room in his shop, all whilst Ingrid sat watching, eyes agog.

She wondered whether to spread a blanket over him, but thought better of it, and instead carried the sleeping Kaja up to the villa and lay down and thought about the last day she had spent with Alexander, in the North Chamber on Barrøy, when they both knew that they would have to tear themselves away from each other, but still hadn't managed to do so, those momentous twenty-four hours, those hours all clock hands had revolved around ever since, those hours that had driven her to embark on this venture which, undeniably, had suffered a setback on the *Munkefjord*, but which now had been restored to full vigour, even though in Skorovas, too, not the slightest trace of him was to be found.

Ingrid believed that her enduring hope was due to the walking, there is life in movement, whether you are Russian or

Norwegian. And she tells Alexander to get up from the chair where he is sitting in her kitchen and walk on his crippled feet, towards the window, to train them, in order for him to become again the man he once was and to be able to get away from here. She watches him totter towards his own reflection in the black glass, then turn and stare at her in despair. She watches him draw a breath and walk towards the pantry door, where he again turns and stares at her with the same doleful desperation in his eyes, a prayer. She rises to her feet and takes him by his bandaged hand and leads him into the hallway and up the stairs and into the North Chamber, and lies with him for the rest of her life.

9

The next evening, too, Benjaminsen drank heavily from the bottle of methylated spirit, and suddenly began to talk about his deceased wife, whom he first claimed he loved, but whom he loved less and less the further into the monologue he got. He burst into tears for no reason – at least as far as Ingrid was able to discern – and never tired of emphasising how happy he was to be in this remote corner of the country, where nobody knew his name.

Ingrid asked what his real name was.

He said with affected laughter that everyone was called Benjaminsen, weren't they, got to his feet, fetched a pot from a grey cupboard and began to piss in it, it took him quite a time.

Ingrid asked what he was thinking of, couldn't he go outside the door or use the privy behind the house?

He could do as he liked in his own shop, couldn't he?

Ingrid said that she was going up to the villa now, to sleep, locks had been fitted to all the doors today.

He said, no, no, wait, and fetched two letters he wanted to show her.

Ingrid could see the sender's name on the back of the envelopes and realised they were from his aforementioned wife, the one who had died, and she said she did not want to read them.

He asked why, wasn't she curious?

"No," Ingrid said, and walked up to the house, locked the doors, and made notes in her sketch pad. Without looking at her childhood drawings this time either, but again she reflected on those last hours with Alexander on Barrøy, the thought of this was not only bearable, it bore her aloft, Alexander in the snow on Barrøy, he wasn't afraid of snow or the low temperatures, he didn't shiver or feel the cold, then she closed her eyes and slept as peacefully as Kaja, her Russian daughter.

The next morning Benjaminsen was sullen and uncommunicative, and didn't remember that he had promised Ingrid payment for helping in the shop. And when she wanted to pay for some milk and bread, he just stood drumming his fingers on the till drawer and staring above her head, as a deep flush rose to the surface of his bearded face.

Ingrid looked intently at him.

He banged the drawer shut and asked her to go outside with him, and as it was broad daylight and he was sober she followed him into the open, where they had a view of the lake and mountains near the entrances to the mines and of the pulsating community, which was growing several centimetres taller with every hour that passed, on either side of the only road that led away from there.

With his back to her, Benjaminsen confessed that he couldn't read.

"Hva?" Ingrid said.

And he just had to know what was in these letters; otherwise he would never have any peace of mind.

Ingrid asked how he could run a shop when he couldn't read.

He said his sons did the bookkeeping, but he couldn't let them read these letters, they were from their mother, to *him*.

Ingrid uttered a hesitant assent, though first she would have to read them alone. He asked her what the point of that was, but made no more of it, and handed her the letters.

Ingrid went up to the villa and into the provisional kitchen, gave Kaja a bottle, and sat down to read a letter which made no mention of any death or illness, but in simple turns of phrase set out how the undersigned Ellisiv was thriving in Bergen in the company of a man both she and Alfred Benjaminsen had obviously known since their childhood.

Nor did the second letter make any mention of an impending death. And its tone was harsh and impatient, as Alfred had obviously not answered the previous letter, Ellisiv wanted to know how her sons were getting on.

Both letters were dated the previous winter, and it was evident from the second that Ellisiv had not only travelled to Bergen on account of her love for this childhood friend of hers, but because Alfred Benjaminsen was given to drink, and violent, in addition he had failed his own country during the war, in ways which at the time might not have been so plain to see, but which were now evident to anyone in their right mind – it was a clear case for the courts.

Ingrid ate two slices of bread and wondered why on earth he had let her read this, went down to the shop again and asked how he could have been married to someone who didn't know he couldn't read?

He didn't understand the question.

Ingrid explained that it wasn't normal to write letters to people who cannot read, and married people would know such things.

"A *can* read," he said wearily. "A bit."

Ingrid asked him why then he had got *her* involved in all this.

He lowered his eyes and said he had hoped she would understand without him having to explain. He needed some advice, for God's sake. He couldn't live without this Ellisiv in Bergen.

Ingrid asked whether fish was all he had sold to the Germans.

His eyes darted around the room and he said yes in a manner which could only mean no.

Ingrid said he was the biggest pillock she had ever met.

He looked at her aghast, then sneered and raised an arm. Ingrid recoiled. And the next moment the door flew open and two men wearing hats and coats entered, a journalist and a photographer Benjaminsen had forgotten he had an appointment with, two men who were going to write an article about the mining community's central role in this new era the country was ushering in, and who had just arrived in a dusty German car, which was parked outside with its engine running. Ingrid hurried out.

The two men stayed in Skorovas for three days. They didn't take any pictures of Benjaminsen, he made sure of that. But one of the photographs which was later to accompany the lengthy article is the only tangible proof that Ingrid Marie Barrøy was staying in Skorovas at this time, with Kaja. In the photograph a woman can be seen walking up the hill from the shore by Lake Litjskorovatn, it is unmistakably Ingrid, with a surprisingly long stride and carrying a child, dressed in a yellow-and-green-striped dress, the colours one can only guess at, it reaches down to just below Ingrid's knees. On her feet she is wearing calf-length boots, which appear to be too big for her, and two lads with close-cropped hair and in short trousers are walk-ing behind her, whilst a man with rolled-up shirtsleeves and wearing a cloth cap and braces is standing outside the newly completed maintenance facilities, looking down on them with a broad smile.

However, it is the repair shop that is the focal point of the photograph. It has just had its roof put on. Two workmen are standing on ladders fitting the drainpipes, and on the ridge of the roof one can just make out the remains of the decorations for a recently held topping-out ceremony. And there is not the slightest sign of what is actually going on in the picture, the search for a missing Russian P.O.W. no-one has heard of in this new Norway.

10

The day after the set-to over the letters, Ingrid awoke determined not to have anything more to do with Benjaminsen and, moreover, felt an alarming twinge of homesickness. The smell of the sea and the sight of people and birds, animals in the meadows, the second summer of peacetime on an island, as different from the first as two seasons, and she wasn't there.

She made sure Kaja was asleep in her cardboard box on the floor, ascertained that the chafing sores she had sustained on her trek across the mountains were healing, and walked barefoot into the cold morning air, where she stood shivering while the half-finished town awakened before her eyes, the columns of smoke rising from one chimney after the other, black figures creeping up the mountainside and into the mine shaft like ants into an anthill. The dwellings of the vast number of people she had talked to and whose names she knew, women and men and children who had begun to treat her like a familiar member of the community, a resident, one of them, as they slowly but surely also forgot why she was actually here, the way everyday life sooner or later will absorb us all, make each one of us ordinary and anonymous, and invisible.

The smell of the sea. The absent sound of birds.

On this day it was nonetheless Benjaminsen – the most indifferent of all to Ingrid's senseless endeavour – who got her started again, by putting her in touch with a mountain farmer who had guided people across the border during the war. Maybe he knows something, Alfred Benjaminsen said out of the blue when Ingrid came into his shop to say goodbye before returning home, she could see he said this with some reluctance, as though he had become resigned to something, a personal defeat.

"Just tha go out an' talk t''im."

Ingrid went outside and encountered Herman Vollheim for the first time. Herman Vollheim was in his mid sixties, he had a square face and a patchy, grey beard and was standing by his tractor gazing sceptically at her with his pale blue eyes as she once again told her story, still falteringly, using words that wouldn't fall into place.

But Herman Vollheim didn't say "what" or "eh?" one single time and also confirmed something Carl's nameless friend, the cargo surveyor in Kongsmoen, had said, that of course refugees used the cableway route, even in winter, they travelled by night, stepping in the footprints of the Bleichert workers, and in so doing left none of their own.

Ingrid nodded.

Vollheim had helped more than a hundred men, women and children over the border to Sweden during the war years, a number of them via the cableway route, yes indeed, but a Russian?

On this point Vollheim, too, was vague and unclear.

Ingrid said that Alexander didn't look like a Russian.

Well, who does? Vollheim laughed sheepishly. The child in her arms did not look Russian either, Kaja, whom Ingrid again held up in the hope that he would recognise her eyes.

"It's a lass."

"Yes, I can see that," Vollheim said.

Ingrid told him about the Russian's charred hands, and Vollheim closed his eyes and pondered, then said, as though something in the deepest recesses of his mind had occurred to him – he wasn't quite sure what – that Ingrid could come and visit him in Stallvika near Lake Tunnsjø in three days, and talk to his daughter, she too had been a courier and guide during the war, she was coming on Saturday.

Ingrid thanked him. And then slept four more nights in the villa, helped Benjaminsen to stack tins and dried food in the storeroom, cleaned the house, and kept his mysterious life at arm's length, as far as this was possible. In addition, she negotiated a pair of shoes in payment, the type the miners wore, the only footwear on sale in Benjaminsen's well-stocked shop, apart from ladies' shoes, of which he did not sell a single pair.

*

Ingrid was also allowed to borrow a bicycle, and was taught how to ride it by his sons.

They were ten and twelve years old, called Trond and Arve, and took it in turns to look after Kaja while Ingrid practised on the bike. And they laughed at her a lot, as she often fell off. They had shaven heads, like war children. And ten-year-old Trond's nose kept bleeding, and he smeared the blood all over his face, dust and dirt stuck to it, only after they had swum in the icy-cold Lake Litjskorovatn did they look like brothers again.

I'll remember these two, as well, thought Ingrid, who was back on the trail, and noted down their names as having significance. She also got each of them to draw a picture for her. Trond drew a horse with legs of somewhat varying lengths and scribbled his name beneath, totally illegible. Arve wrote only his name, in neat handwriting, like an adult's, and Ingrid asked if they missed their mother.

They looked at each other, and Arve solemnly answered "yes" on behalf of them both.

Ingrid regretted she had asked, and told them where she came from, an island in the sea with its own whaler, as well as a number of other boats, four at least.

They eyed her.

Ingrid said that the whaler had a cannon with an iron-tipped harpoon. They nodded. She told them her sister's son was the skipper, his name was Lars. And they asked her to slow down when she talked. Ingrid heaved a sigh of relief and calmly told them about her childhood and the children who were now growing up on the island – whom she must on no account allow herself to miss, she reflected – hoping that they would ask her to stop, but they did not, so she continued talking, and felt homesick for Barrøy. How far she was from home.

It was these two young boys she had been walking up the hill with, on her way to the new repair shop, when she was immortalised in a newspaper photograph. And Ingrid had also swum that day, and dipped Kaja's feet in freshwater. And she learned to ride a bike, thanks not least to Arve, who from her first day in town had followed her with his eyes as though she were his mother, or at least as though Alfred Benjaminsen were not his father.

11

Ingrid Marie Barrøy got up early on Saturday morning, packed and stocked up with food and drink, tied the rucksack onto the bicycle's luggage rack, as Arve had demonstrated, strapped Kaja securely to her belly, and said goodbye to the shopkeeper, who looked as ill-at-ease as Emil Rimala and his first mate, Alf Isaksen, had done when she left the *Munkefjord*, and formally declared that he wished he too had had enough energy to break away from this hellhole.

Ingrid looked down at her new shoes, which were much more comfortable than the boots she had left behind in the villa.

Benjaminsen said that actually he hadn't wanted to put her in touch with Vollheim, she was not to say a word to *anyone* about the shopkeeper in Skorovas, and what he did during the war.

Ingrid said it was peacetime now.

No, it isn't, Benjaminsen snapped, and looked as though he wanted to both embrace her and beat her, but instead turned on his heel and left her to his sons, who stood waiting by the bicycle.

Ingrid got on. The boys took turns at pushing her up the first steep hills and then ran along beside her as far as their strength would allow, Arve furthest, and they shouted in unison that she would have to come back, with the bike.

Balancing on a bike was similar to balancing in a boat, but air is not water, and Ingrid was unsteady and had to get off and wheel it down the steepest slopes, and also when the hills were too steep to ride up.

But Kaja liked being on the bike and laughed in time to its swaying movements. Ingrid turned her to face the dry land-wind, with its dust and pollen, which died down whenever she stopped and they suddenly found themselves in a leaden heat. Then Kaja protested, kicking and crying, but began to laugh again on the next downhill slope. They met three horse-drawn carts and a tractor, Ingrid counted them, passed farms with people working in the fields who raised their tools in a summer greeting, and on a day like today all this could mean was that man is a happy creature in a brave world.

They rested by a river with cold fresh water that sounded like the sea. They ate and drank, and Ingrid sat throwing stones into a whirling eddy until Kaja wanted to get back on the bicycle. She fell asleep as soon as they set off again. Ingrid had become stiff and weary as a result of both the cycling and the rest, so she walked the final kilometre in her new shoes, with Kaja only waking when they arrived at Vollheim farm, which, with its lush, extensive fields, resembled a wide, green hand resting on a hill by the most westerly bay of Tunnsjø, a lake so immense in the mellow afternoon light that the opposite bank was out of sight. It struck Ingrid that there must be even more forest and nothing else over there, and some things are never-ending in this country, and that she was on Alexander's trail.

But Herman Vollheim was standing in his large farmyard with his boots caked in muck and received her with an expression suggesting that he had not been expecting her, or that he was displeased that she had taken him at his word.

Ingrid stood wondering what to do, and gazed across the lake, a breathtaking sight, until he said, wait here, and disappeared into a large, white farmhouse. But he didn't come out again.

Ingrid sat down on the grass.

There were many flowers she had never seen before. And tall unmoving trees It grew darker, the mountain ridges became redder, and Kaja didn't wake up. She wanted to rouse her, but refrained. From inside the house came shouting, silence, then more shouting, which reminded Ingrid of something she had no wish to remember. Eventually the farmhouse door opened, and a small, slender woman came out and stopped beneath the covered veranda with a hand over her eyes, squinting into a sun that was as low as it could be above the land to the west. She walked down the steps and approached Ingrid with tentative steps, and came to a halt three metres in front of her.

Ingrid felt that she might have to shout.

Again there was some "eh"-ing and "what"-ing until they understood each other, by which time Ingrid had gone over and stood beside her.

The woman wasn't so small after all, she had a scar across her left cheek that puckered the corner of her mouth into a smile which wasn't there. And she stared at Ingrid with eyes that were as blue and piercing as those her father must have scrutinised strangers with in his younger days. But she didn't speak his dialect, nor did she look like a guest on the farm, and stretched out her hand and stood holding Ingrid's for so long that Ingrid had to look away.

Her name was Mariann.

Ingrid said her name too, looked straight at her again and explained why she was there, the invisible trail she had followed from the coast, reeled off a long account of how far it was, as though to retain the initiative, and Mariann said she didn't believe a word of it.

Ingrid said, "Hva?"

Mariann rested her eyes on the back of Kaja's sleeping head, and Ingrid decided to ask if she wanted to hold her.

Mariann promptly glanced across the lake, and said, no, and mumbled that she'd had children once herself, a boy and a girl, but they had drowned in the lake, the ice didn't hold. She had also had a husband, whom the Germans had executed in the first year of the war. And she expressed all this in the same short, breathless bursts that Carl with the dog had used when telling of the calamities he had suffered at sea, as though to dispel them from his mind, it was as if a major cleaning-up operation was going on in the country and everyone was involved.

Ingrid had nothing to say to any of this.

Instead, she began to tell Mariann the story of the *Rigel*, the P.O.W. ship the British had bombed eighteen months before, about the Russians who had died and those that had survived, and Mariann said that she had never heard about this, nor did she believe it.

Again Ingrid said, "Hva?"

Mariann shrugged, and Ingrid considered that they had now reached a sufficiently unpleasant state of equilibrium that she could ask to spend the night there, then she would cycle back to Skorovas the following day, they didn't need to give her any food, she was sorry she had come, she should never have done so.

Mariann gave two clear nods, as though to let this sink in, or brush it aside, then turned and began to walk back to the house. But Ingrid had seen her tears. And beneath the veranda roof Mariann turned and stood still, at a distance which made it impossible for them to look each other in the eye. She called across that Ingrid could sleep in the shed down the hill, where the hired haymakers usually stayed, it wasn't locked.

Then Mariann went inside and slammed the door behind her.

Kaja woke up and started crying. Ingrid consoled her, walked down the slope and into the shed, changed and fed her, then played with her until the darkness outside the window could become no redder without going black. They slept in a wide but all too short bed and were awoken by birdsong, the likes of which Ingrid had never heard before, but which was pleasing to lie listening to without moving so much as a finger. In truth, she was lying lifeless and stock-still for fear of breaking the last straw she was clutching at, for fear of crushing something for ever, and terrified that it might be her own fault that she had now reached the end of the road; but Kaja was awake.

12

Ingrid got up and made breakfast from bread and butter and cold tinned food, which was too heavy to carry, no matter whether they would go home or continue. And as they sat eating in the sunshine in front of the shed, Herman Vollheim, the farmer, came along with a small jug of milk in one hand and a pot of steaming coffee in the other, placed both on the doorstep, turned his back to them, looked across the lake and said:

"She was angry, she was. Livid."

Ingrid noticed that he smelled of soap and said she should not have come here, she had said so to Mariann, too.

They both stared at the steaming coffee pot. He swore under his breath and went back to the farmhouse and returned with two cups and asked Ingrid if she hadn't brought any cups with her on the journey.

Ingrid said no, she had woollen blankets, nappies, clothes, food, her father's knife . . .

He said she could keep the one she was holding in her hand, as a souvenir.

Ingrid wondered what kind of souvenir that was supposed to

be, a cup from nowhere, and she said it wasn't necessary, she could buy any she needed, she had more money now than when she left Barrøy.

All right then, he said, and sat down beside her on the sun-warmed rock. They drank their coffee in silence. He suddenly seemed to be in a hurry and said, no, here on the farm the war wasn't over yet, no, got to his feet and went back into the farmhouse with his cup, a completely different person here on the farm from the one he had been in the mining community of Skorovas, two very disparate characters, Ingrid reflected that he was at home in both war and peace and that this wasn't of the slightest use to her.

Now, in the full light of day, she could see across the lake, to the forests on the other side, a velvety, greyish-black wall. There was no wind and the lake was like a mirror. The intense birdsong had changed into short, sharp cries punctuating the day, and two black sails circled above the fields, they looked like eagles.

Ingrid got herself ready, packed, fastened her rucksack to the bike and was about to straddle it when Mariann appeared from behind a fence to the left of the road. She stood with her arms folded and shouted that her father had mentioned a Russian.

Perplexed, Ingrid looked at her and called back that *she*, Ingrid, had already told her about him.

Mariann came closer and said she hadn't taken that in, and added that her father had called Ingrid an idiot and thought she should go back home at once. However, Mariann actually had helped a Russian over the ice a year and a half ago, together with three Norwegian Resistance men, after they had spent a few nights in the boathouse down there, she pointed in the direction of the lake.

Ingrid enquired about his injured hands.

At first, Mariann didn't know what she meant, but then said it was winter, they were wearing mittens.

Ingrid nodded, but didn't move.

Mariann said that they had walked on the ice along the southern bank, heading for the Swedish border, a route she had plotted for them on a map, but she herself hadn't gone with them.

Ingrid let the bicycle fall to the ground, stepped over the ditch and the fence, and held Kaja up to Mariann's face. Mariann recoiled, but stood staring for so long that Ingrid had to lower her eyes, as if she were a child meeting the gaze of an adult. The scar at the corner of Mariann's mouth quivered, she turned and went inside the house.

Ingrid wheeled the bicycle to the haymakers' shed and contemplated the hens strutting around the farmyard. There was a cockerel too. It seemed as though the insects buzzed differently from the way they did on the islands. Kaja scrabbled after the hens, which cackled and scampered off, like the eider ducks on Barrøy. Ingrid sat down. An hour passed. Two. Mariann returned with a map and more coffee. By now the sun was in the south.

Ingrid said that she already had a map.

"Not this one," Mariann said drily.

Then she said that Ingrid could sleep in the farmhouse the following night, they also had a cradle for the child.

Ingrid thanked her, and motioned towards the grass.

Mariann sat down on the ground beside her. They looked at the map, Mariann's slender finger with a filed, pink nail directed at a small cross, which marked a chapel at the easternmost end of Tunnsjø, and a road up through a valley towards Sweden, where another lake stretched further inland, then her finger suddenly began to tremble, and Mariann's voice cursed the lake she said she was doomed to stare at every single morning, every single day, in the summer at night, too.

Ingrid said, no, she wasn't . . .

Mariann said, yes, she was, that was why she lived here and didn't teach in the town, as she once had done, could she hold Kaja?

Ingrid passed Kaja to her, who looked anxiously at the stranger and stuck a fist in her mouth.

"Tha's still young," Ingrid said.

"No, I'm not," Mariann said, without taking her eyes off Kaja.

Ingrid insisted that she couldn't be much older than herself. But Mariann seemed not to hear. She had made Kaja laugh and asked how old her child was. Ingrid told her, and Mariann said, yes, she should have been able to see that herself, what was all this about the *Rigel*?

Ingrid started to tell her, but she didn't get very far this time either before Mariann interrupted her and said this could be a good opportunity to get the boat out again, it had been under cover for over two years.

"The boat?"

Mariann nodded towards the boathouse in the bay.

Ingrid nodded too, as if she understood, and asked how Mariann could be so sure he was a Russian and not a German, a deserter.

Mariann lifted Kaja above her head, jiggled her from side to side in a mother's deft hands and said that she could hear the difference between German and Russian. And now Ingrid had nothing further to ask. She stared in the direction of the boat-house, which stood between two colossal birches that cast long shadows up towards the farm, two identically shaped, greyish-green prisms, and, in the sunlight between them, at all the glittering insects she had never set eyes on before.

13

Ingrid was standing in the kitchen watching Mariann Vollheim making chicken casserole in a black cast-iron pot on an electric stove with four hotplates of different sizes, while Kaja was playing on the floor with a spoon which she had been allowed to bang on a saucepan lid. Ingrid brought up the matter of Herman calling her an idiot, and asked whether Mariann thought that others she had met on her way might have been of the same opinion.

Mariann didn't answer.

Ingrid repeated the question: what did people think of her?

Mariann still didn't reply, but asked Ingrid if she'd had any bad experiences on the way.

Ingrid said, no, folk had been fine, though some children had thrown stones at her bicycle yesterday, and shouted *gippo*, as far as she could make out.

Mariann didn't comment on this, either.

Ingrid asked her to say something.

Mariann gave a quick smile and said that if anyone had searched as intensely for *her* as Ingrid had done for this Russian, lots of things would have been different.

Ingrid reflected on this.

Mariann said it was of no relevance what *she* thought, but what she would like to say was that her own children would never be coming back. She would also like to say their names aloud, but she couldn't, she hadn't been able to since they died, not even at the funeral.

Ingrid asked if they had gone to school.

"Yes. They were seven and nine. It happened at Christmas four years ago, just after they'd lost their father." It was only later that Mariann had decided to join the Resistance, like Herman, in order to survive, before that she hadn't even known what he was up to.

Ingrid said she had only one child, Kaja, and Mariann didn't comment.

They took turns to stir the casserole with a ladle.

Ingrid tasted it and suggested adding more salt.

"Over there," Mariann said, pointing with her ladle in the direction of a salt cellar.

"Ya, does tha think A should put meir in?" Ingrid insisted.

"Yes," Mariann said, sitting down on a chair. Ingrid sprinkled in a little more salt, stirred and tasted. Mariann leaned over the tabletop, pressed her face against a tea towel, got to her feet, put her hands on her hips and announced through a window, which was open on this summer evening, that her children's names were Herman and Selma.

*

They ate in silence at a long dining table in a large room which could accommodate many more people. Kaja sat in a chair that had been specially made for a child. Mariann fed her with the same food that the adults had. Ingrid said that Kaja might also like a little milk. Herman asked her how far she had walked. Ingrid told him about the fishing boat from Innøyr and the *Munkefjord* and about the many kilometres she had travelled on foot from Kongsmoen to Skorovas. And he apologised.

Mariann looked up from Kaja's bowl, which had also been specially made for a child, it was wooden, and she said *he* was the idiot.

Ingrid giggled behind her hand and asked how they made the juice she was drinking, was it redcurrant?

"Raspberry," Mariann said, and began to question her about Barrøy and the *Rigel* and all the things she hadn't taken in when Ingrid told her the first time. Ingrid talked on about whatever came to mind, and finished by saying it was strange being here, now all the windows were open and there was not a sound to be heard.

For breakfast she was given a fried egg and pork and bread. Mariann fed Kaja again, this time with porridge oats, soured milk and honey. Then she got up in the middle of the meal and left. Ingrid didn't know what to say to Herman, who sat bent over his fried egg in what appeared to be deep thought. He was wearing a white shirt and embroidered braces, but was otherwise dressed in rough working clothes. Now, too, he smelled of carbolic soap, and there was an embarrassed expression in those sky-blue eyes of his that made him seem so much younger than he was. Then, without warning, he said it was good to have Ingrid there, not to her face, but to a wall, which was covered in rustic wallpaper with cascading vines in shades of pale pink and green, and it didn't seem as though he meant what he said.

Ingrid said he had a fine farm.

"Yes," he said.

Ingrid asked if he had any children apart from Mariann.

"Yes, two boys, one in Trondheim and one in America. That one's a soldier."

They carried on eating, and he put down his knife and fork with such a clatter it could have been heard on Barrøy, got to his feet, went over to the electric cooker, fetched the pot of coffee and poured some for Ingrid, then sat down again, took a deep breath and looked as if he were about to utter all the words that exist in a language, but not a sound passed his lips.

When Kaja had eaten her fill, Ingrid cleared the table, as though she lived there, and prepared to wash up. Herman rose to his feet, too, and said that he had never experienced anything like this in his life.

But his tone was gentle. He stroked Kaja's cheek with a rough, tanned hand covered in prominent veins, causing her to look up at him, and he said, like a foreman to a subordinate, well, now he'd better be off into the forest and make himself useful, everything was getting overgrown.

When Ingrid had packed and come out into the farmyard with Kaja in her arms, Mariann was waiting for her. It was early in the season and the grass was short here in the mountains, but with her were two haymakers, who looked as if they were brothers and in their black breeches and red-checked flannel shirts resembled tin soldiers. Mariann asked what Ingrid thought they should do with the bicycle. Ingrid said she hadn't given it a thought, it belonged to Benjaminsen, who had a shop in Skorovas.

"So you aren't thinking of going back?" Mariann said. "Back home?"

"No," Ingrid said.

Mariann said her father could return the bicycle to Skorovas on his tractor, took Kaja in her arms, and told Ingrid to follow.

One of the tin soldiers grabbed her rucksack, so Ingrid could walk without encumbrance, like a guest of honour, down the slope between the two birch trees that looked like dark clouds and eventually filled the whole sky. The boathouse was larger than it appeared from up at the farm and stood absurdly far out in the water.

The two haymakers opened the doors and winched out a vessel more than twenty feet long, which was not unlike a white clog and immediately began to take in water.

Ingrid said they had forgotten to put in the drain plug.

Mariann laughed, took a few steps to the side with Kaja and pointed at some ducks circling around in the reeds just off the shore. The men bailed out the water and cranked up the engine and got it started. It emitted some black puffs of smoke and died again. Ingrid sat down in the grass; the ducks reminded her of the eiders, but they were smaller, with blue and brown heads, and they didn't coo. Some large white flowers were floating on the water, along the banks reeds and leaves and semi-rotten pieces of wood were bobbing up and down in a film of yellow pollen.

Mariann sat beside her and asked if she missed Barrøy. Ingrid said, no, it was impossible for her to be there *now*, an answer it struck her she couldn't have given more clearly and unequivocally at any other time previously, not even when she left Malvika, it couldn't have been stated more emphatically, at any rate, than now.

"And what if you don't find anything?" Mariann said.

"Any*thing*?" Ingrid said. And they said no more.

The two hired hands got the engine started again. It spluttered, then began to spew first blue, then white smoke from its exhaust pipe behind the stern. The sound became as soft and rhythmic as a deer's heart. From down between the shady birches came Herman Vollheim, carrying an empty coffee cup, which he handed to Ingrid as if it were of no value. She examined it closely and saw that it was daintier than the one she had drunk from the previous morning, when he had sat with her in front of the haymakers' shed. She thanked him and put it in her rucksack, picked up Kaja, and stepped aboard.

There were no thwarts in the boat, but benches along the sides. She sat with her feet on the engine casing, it was vibrating. Next to it stood a blue wooden crate, like a Lofoten chest, except that it was square and had wrought-iron handles.

Mariann stepped on board, too, and sat on the bench along the opposite side to keep the boat balanced. One of the haymakers sat at the helm in the stern, and the other at the front in the forepeak. The helmsman engaged the clutch, the vessel made a gentle curve across the bay, then headed due east. They waved to Herman Vollheim, and Ingrid asked if they were going far.

Mariann said a little more than twenty kilometres. Her hands rested on top of the folded map on her knees, and she had a compass on a string around her neck. Ingrid studied it intently, but did not recognise it.

Tunnsjø is a monster of a lake, which only reveals its true self when you leave the bays behind and see the island mountain which towers up in its midst, Gudfjelløya, five hundred metres of bluish-black rock above the waterline, an island that grows bigger the closer one gets to it and suddenly becomes gigantic when single trees can be picked out in the elm forest on the southern wall and they appear no bigger than matchsticks.

Mariann shouted above the drone of the engine and pointed.

The helmsman changed course and followed the headlands shorewards. Ingrid spotted a tiny farm at the foot of the island mountain, which now resembled a bank of cloud, and the farm disappeared. She leaned over the side and scooped up some water and drank, laughed and repeated the process. Mariann asked what she was doing. Ingrid shook her head good-humouredly and splashed Kaja, making her laugh too. She also gave her some water to drink, and the hours passed with the mountainous rock still in view.

They stepped ashore at the easternmost end of the lake, left the boat in the care of the haymakers, and scrambled up through a rustling birch forest into a churchyard adjacent to the small chapel they had seen on the map, surrounded by a moss-covered wall and long, motionless grass. The sweet smell of earth and heavy forest filled the air. Mariann tried the door of the white building, it was locked. She said it had always been open during the war, so couriers and refugees could spend the night there, there was a stove in the vestry. Then out of the blue she asked if Ingrid had a watch.

Ingrid said no.

Mariann pulled out a small, flat cardboard box, opened it, dangled a man's watch from her right forefinger and handed it to Ingrid. She was standing one step above her when she did this, and said that she had set it this morning, it had to be wound every day.

Ingrid said she couldn't accept it, it was too valuable.

Mariann said, yes, it was valuable, so she would have to bring it back when she returned, it had belonged to Herman's father.

They smiled at one another, and Mariann said she would show her the way after they had eaten.

They sat in the grass with their backs to the wall, which Ingrid discovered was overgrown with creeping rose root, a sea plant. She explained that this plant didn't belong here, nor did she and Kaja, a comment which Mariann either didn't hear or didn't understand, in the same way that she herself hadn't understood freshwater, how strange it is to find yourself in a boat sailing on water you can drink.

Mariann told her there was yet another lake further inland, which they called Little Tunnsjø, a narrow appendix which reached almost to the border, where there was a cabin that was also used during the war.

"Ah ya?" Ingrid said with interest.

Mariann said it was strange being in this place again, now when there was nothing to fear, it was the first time for many years that she could hear the hush here, a silence she apparently wanted to say more about, if only she could have found the words, or the strength, but she could not, and Ingrid felt compelled to say she understood what she meant.

Mariann walked ahead of her down to the bank and said that the two men should try to manoeuvre the boat through the connecting stretch of water. They said in unison that this was out of the question, she could see that for herself.

Mariann said it didn't matter, there was another boat in Little Tunnsjø.

She led them across a narrow isthmus, where a small rowing boat came into view beneath a dense thicket. It was lying belly up. They got it in the water and stepped aboard. Ingrid and Mariann sat on the stern thwart taking it in turns to have Kaja on their lap, while the men rowed across black water into a green evening, through a channel which became so narrow that the blades of their oars dragged through reeds and water lilies, into an even more constricted part of the inlet, with leaves hanging so densely above the surface of the water that the cabin Mariann had mentioned didn't become visible until the iron keel bumped against the boulders on the shore.

The cabin was unlocked, alongside the walls there were plank beds covered in reindeer skins, a table screwed to the floor, a small stove and some empty bookcases with people's names carved into the uprights. A low door led into another room. Mariann sat down. One of the tin soldiers said they had to be off, evening was drawing in.

Mariann said they were going to spend the night here, there was food and blankets in the wooden chest, tomorrow she would accompany Ingrid across the border into Sweden, and only then would she return to Vollheim.

The other tin soldier asked crossly why she hadn't said

anything before they set out, they only had today, they were building a house in Skorovas. And Mariann said she hadn't made up her mind until now.

The first man muttered then why had she brought along so much food and all these blankets?

Mariann didn't answer. She said the two of them could sleep in there, and pointed to the door of the back room, while she and Ingrid would bed down here next to the stove, it would do them no harm. The men looked at each other in despair and went out to pull the boat ashore and fetch the blue chest.

Ingrid asked when Mariann had changed her mind.

"In the churchyard."

Ingrid asked if that was where her children had been laid to rest.

"Yes."

Ingrid pondered for a moment, then said she would like to thank her. But Mariann had turned her back and was picking kindling from a bin, some sheets of yellowed newspaper, a few logs, she knelt down in front of the stove while Ingrid laid Kaja on a reindeer skin, changed her, lay down beside her and closed her eyes. She sensed that Kaja had closed her eyes too. She heard the crackling in the stove and Mariann ordering the men to fetch more wood and fill the water buckets. Without opening her eyes, Ingrid asked if Alexander had spent the night here.

"Here or in the chapel," Mariann said, and added that it would probably have taken them a good twenty-four hours to cross the ice, there was a lot of snow. But she imagined the next stage of their journey had been even harder, they would find out more about all this tomorrow.

Ingrid asked if she could have something to drink.

Mariann told her to help herself, the ladle and buckets were on the bench next to her.

"Reit," Ingrid said, and fell asleep.

14

From the burlap sack on which she was resting her head, Ingrid could see Kaja's dark locks, Kaja, who was lying beside her under a grey woollen blanket which someone had spread over them. The sunlight trickled through the cracks in the rotting door, illuminating dancing insects and dust. A mouse darted across the floor. The roof beams above her were covered in names and initials. She didn't find what she was looking for and wondered whether she herself would have left any trace of her presence if she had been in Alexander's shoes, a trail which could be followed by both friend and foe, the same question she had asked herself every time she encountered someone who didn't remember, had he not left a single clue behind him, deliberately? And she also wondered at the fact that she had continued her quest, without really having decided to do so, no matter what answers people had given her. She came to the conclusion that there being no trace of him was a good sign, but *she* would have carved *her* name in one of these beams, made her presence here known and maybe even have added some telling words, it was such a short distance to freedom, an unequivocal signal to the person who might be following and in need of this sign of life more than anything else. But then it occurred to her that *she* was perhaps not like him, and felt a strange sense of disappointment as Mariann mumbled from where she was lying:

"You're worn out. Can you carry on today?"

"Yes."

"Remember to wind the watch, make a habit of it, every morning."

Ingrid rolled onto her back, got out the watch, turned the tiny knob, and asked Mariann if she'd had any contact since then with any of the three men who accompanied her Russian across the ice, and why didn't she call him Alexander, after all she knew very well what his name was?

Mariann said no.

Ingrid asked why not.

Mariann said that of all the men she had helped over the border during those two years she had been active she had only met one again, and she had received four letters of thanks, she hadn't heard a word from the other thirty-seven, probably they wanted to forget both her and the war.

"Else they'r dead," Ingrid said.

Mariann didn't answer, and Ingrid asked if she recognised any of the names on the beams or the bookcase. Mariann came over and lay down beside her, and read them, and said, yes, that one there, and that one, and *him*, he was no more than sixteen, one of the four who had written to thank her. Then she said she knew what was on Ingrid's mind and that she should think about something else.

They made some food and ate it to the sound of snoring from the next room, in what Ingrid considered would have been an oppressive atmosphere, had they not had Kaja, who was sitting on the table between them and laughing at their playful fingers, she was so serenely marble-white and oblivious to both war and peace that Ingrid was able to reassure herself – once again – that the journey had not only been undertaken because of Kaja, it couldn't even have happened without her, without a child to lug around, this most divine of all burdens.

They left the cabin without waking the men, Mariann carrying Ingrid's rucksack and Ingrid with Kaja, following a winding, dusty road leading east, and they met no-one until Mariann declared that now we are in Sweden.

Ingrid cast an eye around the scrub and said there wasn't much of a border.

Mariann nodded at a yellow sign, which looked as though it had been peppered by innumerable shotgun pellets.

They continued for another five kilometres along the same road, still without meeting anyone, and stopped in front of a red-walled house with a covered veranda, a hipped roof, and five pairs of shoes of different sizes, arranged neatly on either side of the lowest step of the staircase.

Mariann told Ingrid to wait, and went inside.

Ingrid walked around the closely cropped lawn, listening to the sheep bells and gazing out across a lake that was just as immense as Tunnsjø, but without a magical mountain. Mariann came out again accompanied by a young man with a sleepy face and two lengths of rope holding up his trousers. He stuck his bare feet into the largest of the shoes, blew his nose into his hand and stepped aside as Mariann explained to Ingrid that there had been a hitch, the man they had been going to talk to died last winter, this is his son, Nils.

Ingrid asked what they were going to do then.

Mariann said that now they wouldn't be able to meet the courier with whom she and her father had worked. But they had reached the banks of Lake Kvarnberg, and Nils had said he was willing to ferry her over to Gäddede, the nearest populated area, where the regional public prosecutor resided during the war, as well as the man who had taken in the four refugees and hopefully helped them further on their way, for a small fee, twenty kroner, Norwegian.

Ingrid gave a start when she realised that this was the price *she* had to pay for the transport.

"He's Swedish," Mariann said.

Ingrid enquired if she could make it on foot.

Mariann said the road was terrible, and it was more than fifty kilometres, not only that, rain was on the way.

Ingrid gave this some thought, then asked Mariann if she

had come all this way only to persuade her to go back home with her, and give up, that was how it seemed.

With an indeterminate expression on her face, Mariann said that that, at any rate, was what her father hoped.

"Hva?" Ingrid said.

Mariann said she was wondering whether to give Ingrid some money to cover the transport, or to go with her, but she wasn't up to it.

"Tha isn't up t' hva?"

Mariann mumbled something she didn't understand, and Ingrid hastened to say that she hadn't spent much of the money from the eider down they had sold, and she had also earned a few kroner at Benjaminsen's, not to mention the money she got from the sale of the suitcase.

Again Mariann said nothing.

Ingrid felt that the decision was not only *hers* to take, but that it on no account should be Mariann's.

"A've got Kaja," she said.

"Yes, I know," Mariann said, to the grass.

Ingrid asked if she could trust Nils.

Mariann said that his father had been a good man.

"So, what have you decided?"

Yes, Ingrid would carry on, nothing can end like this.

Mariann went over and exchanged a few words with Nils, came back and said he wanted the money immediately, but Ingrid shouldn't agree to that.

Ingrid walked over to Nils and said he could have ten kroner now, and ten when they got there.

Nils' face turned red and he shot an enquiring glance at Mariann, who failed to come to his rescue.

Ingrid said she could show him the other ten, so he could be sure she had it.

Nils said in his language that he didn't understand. Mariann shouted something Ingrid didn't understand either, and Nils still looked sceptical.

Ingrid asked why *she* should trust him when *he* didn't trust her.

Mariann laughed and translated, and Nils considered it an opportune moment to bend down and pick up a blade of grass and chew on it.

Ingrid asked if he wasn't going to put on some socks.

He looked quizzically at Mariann, who didn't translate, instead she turned away and laughed, Ingrid could see that from her heaving back, beneath a cardigan which Mariann had told her the previous day that she had knitted for her father, but which was too small for him. Now Ingrid also noticed that she had freckles on the side of her neck, in the light that fell on them from between the dark clouds that had drifted in over the lake and turned it grey. She also noticed that despite the small scar on her face she was a beautiful woman, a beautiful woman who didn't know it and never would.

"Shall we bi goen?" she said to Nils.

15

The rain beat down on them like yammering thunder. Ingrid draped an oilskin over herself, which was big enough to cover Kaja, too, and sat with her knees pressed together, humming monotonously to the rhythm of the engine struggling through the water. Nils was wearing a thick woollen cardigan over his boiler-suit, shoes without socks, his hair plastered flat against an oddly shaped skull, and he didn't say a word.

The enormous lake blended in with the forests, which came and went like distant carpets of grey as Ingrid thought about when she and Mariann had said goodbye, standing on the banks, and how Mariann, obviously unused to touching another person, at the critical moment had laid a hand on her shoulder, presumably this was meant to be a final warning, but it went unheeded.

Ingrid saw herself – sitting shivering in a white Swedish boat with tar-brown gunwales and thwarts and an outboard motor that was only just managing to groan and growl its way forward through the driving rain, the grey mat of nails, in a boundless wilderness, zero visibility in all directions. She watched the water swell and wash over the floorboards but said nothing, and Nils didn't react. She heard Mariann's cries as they set off, about a man she should see in Gäddede, in a green brick house in Solvegen with flowers in the front window, she didn't remember the number, only the flowers, and don't forget to read the notes on the sheet of paper, the sheet of paper she had given her.

Roughly halfway across the lake Kaja began to whine. Nils appeared to take this as a bad omen, opened his mouth and presumably shouted that this couldn't go on. The next moment he throttled down and they came to a standstill in rain that showed not the least sign of abating.

Ingrid shouted in her dialect that there was a pump over by the port gunwale.

He put his hand on the brass cylinder and said, she supposed, that it didn't work.

Ingrid leaned forward and pulled at the T-bar, not a drop came out.

There was no wind, the silence was deafening, no land in sight. Nils revved up the engine and changed course. Only minutes later they glided into a stony bay, where a timber hay barn came into view in the bushes, the size of the tallest buildings they had on the small islands in the sea. Nils went ashore and helped Ingrid with her rucksack and Kaja, who was now screaming at the top of her voice.

There was no stove in the barn, but some relatively dry hay; from a nail hung a soot-covered coffee pot; some old reindeer hides were spread over a rotting hatch that turned out to be the remains of the front door, at the far end the roof was leaking.

Ingrid put some dry clothes on Kaja and consoled her and discovered all too late that, outside, the engine had been started up again. She didn't go out to watch the boat vanish into the distance, for some reason she knew that it was gone for ever.

The eaves projected over the door-less opening. Ingrid managed to light a fire with some dry hay and logs she found lying around. She checked that the smoke wasn't drifting into the building, and for the first time since she had left Barrøy she could feel that she was afraid.

Ingrid Marie Barrøy had been afraid before, at sea, many times, but there was a good reason for that, here there was just rain and the desolate wastelands.

She got out Kaja's rag doll, called Bonken after a cat they had once had on Barrøy, and put it in her lap. Kaja's face lit up and she grabbed it with both hands. She made what appeared to be a bed for it in the hay, then covered it, or was she burying it?

Ingrid kept the fire going and tried to dry their clothes. She heated some water in the coffee pot and made some food, got out the map Mariann had given her, as well as the sheet of paper on which she, sure enough, had written two names and where

Ingrid could find these people in this community with the impossible name. She had also included her own postal address, but nothing else, and Ingrid thought this very little. She read the note three times, and that was all there was.

16

Ingrid lay awake until the rain let up at around midnight, leaving a calm which was no more reassuring than the noise. She put more wood on the fire and slept restlessly beneath the damp blankets, and was woken by the rays of the sun striking her face. She pressed her cheek against Kaja's chest to listen to her breathing, sat up, wound Herman Vollheim's watch and made something to eat while Kaja was coming to – in one long stretch, and she set off walking.

A path of sorts led from the lake up to the road Ingrid had picked out on the map. She waited until the quivering needle on Mariann's compass had made up its mind, then headed east without a thought in her head and walked for the rest of the day on gravel which gradually turned to dust, with low, dense forest on either side, through a tunnel of foliage, the blue sky like a canopy above.

And now she was no longer light of foot, but flustered and agitated, like a fugitive. And Kaja was no longer a god-given burden, but a living well-spring of wails and howls. They made their way through the tunnel that was so straight and endless that her walking took them neither forwards nor backwards. Ingrid stopped, looked around in the undergrowth, and went on, stopped again and washed nappies in a black stream, but found no peace of mind.

She hung the nappies from her rucksack like flags and walked on until a hazy objective became visible in the far distance. But it was just a sharp bend which led into a new and similarly endless corridor. She sat down once more and ate quickly and frenetically. Kaja began to wail again. Ingrid packed her things and walked on in seething swarms of midges, defiantly picking a path through a labyrinth that was as straight as an arrow, and all directions ceased to exist. Her pulse was out of control. The sweat poured down her. She swatted away insects and protected Kaja with a wet nappy and saw the same unbending road both behind and in front of her. There was panic in every step she took, and she was about to burst into tears when a solitary farm appeared out of nowhere and she gave a start. Two red buildings. But no sign of people.

She trudged on and rounded two more bends and came upon another farm, larger than the first, with a couple of shadowy figures at the edge of the forest above an unpainted barn. She continued and heard the whine of a lumber saw. The forest shrank and tapered into fields. Above them, birds hovered. A couple of horses came wading through a meadow of flowers and stuck their heads over a dilapidated fence so that Ingrid was able to stroke two muzzles and feel the warmth of animals and realise that she had arrived, and now Kaja was no longer crying.

Ingrid had been walking for more than eight hours, her feet were aching and Kaja's weight was enough to make anyone's knees give way as she staggered warily into a box-like cluster of buildings arranged around two roads that crossed at right angles, there was not a soul to be seen. On some high ground west of the crossroads towered a majestic church, encircled by equally majestic trees, and everything seemed to be at rest, dormant, at the foot of this celestial monument that drew Ingrid towards it like a magnet.

With a final burst of energy, she walked up the slope and into the graveyard with a well-tended flower bed, unlike anything she had ever seen or imagined – the black and white stone-teeth, the crosses and the faceless names and dates. She sat down and leaned back against a slab of slate, turned Kaja away to avoid her gaze, and closed her eyes.

When she opened them again, the sun hung low over the mountaintops in her homeland, hovering above the trimmed hedge to the west. A white sign bore the name Frostviken, the salvation of not only Ingrid and Kaja, but also of three Norwegian Resistance men and a Russian P.O.W. with mangled hands, an engineer from Leningrad. It was now 579 days since Ingrid had lain in the North Chamber holding his crippled hands in hers, this was an uplifting thought here in the first breathing space she'd had on the journey, now she could also look Kaja in the eye again, and she knew that she had been asleep without being aware of it.

She got to her feet, walked back down to the village and knocked on the first door, there was no answer and she went to the next. She was told where she could buy food, but not today, it was closed. She carried on until she spotted some flowers in the windows of a green brick-house with its roof and walls in a poor state of repair, knocked on the door there, too, and nobody answered. She knocked again, heard heavy footsteps and watched as a chink of light appeared in the doorway. Two eyes at knee-height studied her, a voice said something she didn't understand. Ingrid introduced herself and explained why she was there. The door slammed shut and she heard some shouting, a man's voice. Then there was silence. She knocked again, harder, fiercely, with both hands until she could no longer recognise herself, then went back to the house where she had been told that the store was closed, and enquired where the doctor, David Hübner, lived, the second name on Mariann's piece of paper.

She was directed to the last house down one road, a red, two-storey residence with a hipped roof and dormer, newly painted windows and barge-boards, standing behind a grassy stone wall where there was a road sign pointing to Norway. Inside the grounds stood an enormous tree, its branches hanging so closely above the house that it looked as though it was holding its hand over it.

Once more, Ingrid knocked at the door.

A burly woman in her fifties opened up, she was dressed all in white like a nurse or a cook and had big, friendly eyes with a slight squint in the right one, a few auburn locks protruded from beneath a bonnet which was even whiter than her uniform.

She didn't understand what Ingrid said, but gabbled a number of phrases, all presumably in Swedish and including the word *läkaren*, he was *upptagen* just at the minute, and she asked if the child was *sjukt*, which Ingrid did understand and to which she answered "no".

"No?" the woman repeated, before disappearing inside.

Ingrid heard a key being turned in the lock, and knew that she had finally reached the end of the road. She went back down the steps and sat on a bench beneath the tree, with Kaja on her lap, she gave her some food and the rest of the milk. She herself didn't eat, but played with Kaja and Bonken, her rag doll, until she fell asleep in her arms.

It began to rain again.

Ingrid draped the oilskins over them and sat waiting, grateful for every minute that Kaja didn't wake up. She heard a window open behind her and a voice call out. She did not turn and did not answer. Soon afterwards, the door opened and she heard heavy footsteps on the gravel. A middle-aged man in a brown woollen suit, white shirt and blue tie stood before her, one hand in his pocket, the other ready to shake hers. He asked her in Norwegian what she wanted.

Once again, Ingrid began to tell her story, but halted even before she had properly got going, fell quiet and looked away for fear of bursting into tears. He stood watching, and after a while said:

"Try again."

Ingrid tried again. At length he stuck his other hand in his pocket and rocked on the soles of his feet as she concluded her story, quickly put his hand to his chin and said she had better come inside.

"I'll take your rucksack."

Ingrid entered a dark hallway with a crystal chandelier hanging from the ceiling and photographs in black, oval frames on the walls, and was led along a wall-papered corridor which opened into a room with books on three walls and a brick hearth in the fourth, the fire was lit.

Hübner motioned to her to take a seat and said that Sabine would be coming with some food, then sat down in the other armchair, beside a round table, and stared straight ahead for so long that Ingrid felt she ought to say something, if only to rouse him.

She enquired about the green house with the flowers in the window.

Hübner said Nikolas lived there, the poor devil, and continued to sit in silence until Sabine came in with a tray of open sandwiches, cups and a pot of steaming coffee, and said that

Ingrid should take off her oilskins and also the sweater which became visible after she had done so, and put on the woollen socks she handed her, and – what about the child, does she want some milk, she asked in Swedish.

Ingrid nodded her thanks and watched as the clothes disappeared out of the door with Sabine, who closed it after her like the lid of a jewellery case. Hübner opened his mouth and announced that Ingrid probably wasn't going to like what he was about to tell her, but he would do so nonetheless, as though his account was lent more gravity as a consequence of these expressed misgivings.

What had happened was that when the four refugees were supposed to make their way from Vollheim across Lake Tunnsjø there was so much snow that they arrived late for their rendezvous with Nikolas on the Swedish side, he had turned round and gone home again.

Ingrid looked at him.

The Norwegians had decided to carry on all the same, even though none of them was familiar with the terrain, and eventually came across a cabin near Lake Kvarnberg. They were found there by Nikolas the following day, in a fairly bad state. Nikolas, however, suspected that one of them might be a German agent, and refused to help them on their way.

Ingrid looked at him.

Hübner said that the Norwegians were furious and attacked Nikolas, but he managed to get away.

"And?" Ingrid said.

Hübner took a deep breath and said that what happened later he had only found out after the war, as Nikolas said no more about these goings-on except that the Norwegians hadn't turned up for the first rendezvous.

Ingrid felt like saying "And?" again.

But one day last autumn one of the Resistance men came here to Gäddede and beat the living daylights out of Nikolas in his own home, with a hammer, he held him responsible for them losing a good comrade. Because after the trouble at Lake Kvarnberg the four of them had gone back to Tunnsjø, you see, and from there made their way south across the mountains on the Norwegian side of the border until they came to a farm called Kleiva, where they were helped by some Norwegians.

"But when they arrived, there were only three of them," Hübner said solemnly, glancing at Ingrid, then said by way of conclusion that she could relax, her Russian was among the survivors, and that's all I know.

Ingrid chewed slowly on her slices of bread, fed Kaja and asked Hübner how well he knew Mariann and Herman Vollheim.

"Extremely well," he said, they had worked together through-out the war, Herman had made more than fifty trips across Lake Tunnsjø, mostly in a rowing boat, he had saved countless lives, Mariann too.

Ingrid asked if he thought Herman and Mariann knew about this misunderstanding between the refugees and Nikolas.

"I doubt it," Hübner said, breaking into Swedish. "But I can't be sure."

Ingrid asked if he thought that she, with all these evasive answers, would ever get to know the truth.

He was taken aback, and pondered on this, as though to give her time to regret what she had said – which she made no sign of doing – and then said in a peremptory tone:

"You're walking along a road of bad consciences, my dear."

"Hva?" Ingrid said.

Hübner answered – as far as she could make out – that the Occupation of Norway had been of a special kind, in many places it had been more like co-operation, it had tainted people, now they were washing away the stains, the country is cleaning its hands. Yes, even many of those who did do something of value know that they could have done more, and they would prefer not to be reminded of it.

Ingrid considered this and felt it made sense. She said she was glad he had told her what he knew.

Hübner said she didn't look glad.

She ignored this and said she had been afraid today, but was no longer. Had Hübner heard any more about her Russian?

"Not really," he said evasively. He said that the three survivors who had made it south to the village of Nordli had been taken care of by another courier. Ingrid could have his name and address. Hübner could also arrange transport to this place for her the following morning.

"In Norway?"

"Yes, Norway."

Ingrid thanked him again and asked if he thought everyone she had met on her way had been pulling the wool over her eyes like this.

He peered up at her in surprise and this time made no attempt to make her feel regret for what she had said, and exclaimed:

"You're unbelievable."

Ingrid asked what he meant by: You're unbelievable.

Ingrid said what people had been telling her was a load of rubbish, and asked what *he* thought about her suspicions.

He smiled and threw out his arms.

"I think you're right!"

Ingrid asked how much he wanted for the transport to Nordli, and if she could stay the night in his house, and what *that* would cost. As he didn't answer, she asked him whether he had heard of the *Rigel*. Hübner hadn't. Yet another who hadn't.

17

There was no chance to say goodbye to the doctor the following day, he was busy with patients. Ingrid awoke rested but stiff, with a lingering tinge of fear as a consequence of the forest and the rain, and needed to get up and feel the cold floor beneath the soles of her feet.

Kaja was awake, sitting up in the elegantly crafted cot playing with Bonken. Ingrid lifted her up and said that now it's only two months until you are one year old, my girl, you'll have to start walking, I learned when I was ten months old, Lars when he was only seven months . . .

The over-furnished room had heavy curtains that were tied at the waist, making Ingrid think of other women than herself, and they only allowed a glimpse onto the closely cropped lawn and two straight lines of soft-fruit bushes which stretched as far as the eye could see – there was nothing left for her to do but change Kaja, dress her, and herself, and wind Herman Vollheim's watch.

Sabine had prepared breakfast. She ate with them, and talked continuously between mouthfuls, regardless of whether Ingrid understood or not, the most important thing, it seemed, was that something was said. And Ingrid reflected that there was no evil in Sabine, but she had her faults too, it was as though she were talking about what she was talking about to avoid talking about something else, her words were like rocks in a dam which on no account could be allowed to burst.

But during the meal she showed increasing interest in Kaja, babbling to her and chucking her chin, and when it was time for them to leave, as the transport had arrived, she declared – from what Ingrid could make out – that she had never seen such beautiful eyes. It sounded as if saying this gave her some solace, and that was more or less the only hope she felt capable of sending with them on their way from this unreal place, where death appeared to have greater priority than life.

Ingrid climbed up onto the back of a lorry and sat bathed in white sunlight with Kaja in her lap, surrounded by wooden crates full of Swedish tinned food, sacks of sugar and cardboard boxes containing net curtains. To the north of the rumbling vehicle she visualised four refugees fighting their way through a snow-covered wilderness – where now everything was lush and verdant - without food, and one of them succumbing, a Norwegian, while two of his compatriots and a Russian plod on, three men who presumably cannot talk to each other, or rather only two of them, not the Russian, so how do they know they can trust one another, how do they arrive at their decisions . . . ?

They passed a cattle grid, the driver wrenched at the steering wheel like a madman, cursed or cheered in the cab, Ingrid couldn't tell the difference, and Kaja smiled nervously up at her. They were back in Norway, and Ingrid tried to get a sense of this, but felt nothing and realised she would have to resign herself to not understanding why she was doing what she was doing, and not let it worry her, as if it were possible to think in a way which was unthinkable. Or stop feeling what she felt. What are you doing to me, little one, she thought, and pressed Kaja to her body.

They arrived at the village of Nordli in a light drizzle. The driver pointed out the farm of a certain Roald Høgmo, whose name Ingrid had made a note of at the behest of Hübner in Gäddede. And for the first time she felt, so far without any suspicion, that she wasn't received like some insane surprise visitor, but as if she had been expected, by a smiling man in his late forties with a trim black beard, lively, interested eyes, and a missing button from the front of a checked flannel shirt he had carelessly stuffed down the waist of his trousers.

Neither did it occur to her, as he led her past a telephone hanging on the hallway wall, that she had also seen a telephone in Vollheim's house, and of course a doctor would have a telephone too. It only dawned on her when she saw all three of them together, Mariann and Herman Vollheim with Dr Hübner, whose house she had left only a few hours previously – they were sitting around a dining table in a heavy, rustic living room with so many rose-painted cupboards and paraphernalia and furniture stacked up along the walls that it made the place seem like a depository of fine objects for which there was no use.

Roald Høgmo's wife, Katinka, was also present, she greeted Ingrid good-humouredly, and a boy, whom Ingrid took to be the son of the house, a twelve- or thirteen-year-old who stood up as soon as she came in and left with a wry smirk on his face.

Katinka bade Ingrid take a seat, which she hesitated to do, as if to avoid a trap, even though she was unable to guess at what that might be. She sat down nonetheless, placed Kaja on the table in front of her, like some kind of argument, with the feeling that she was facing a tribunal consisting of familiar, but evasive masks, each of them unsuccessfully trying to make her feel at ease.

Mariann did not look at her, even though Ingrid had no difficulty looking at *her*. Herman Vollheim had conjured up a new smile, which did not become him, even though his blue eyes were as boyish as ever. And Hübner, the doctor, appeared to have resumed the silent examination he had engaged in the previous evening, an examination of the case of Ingrid Marie Barrøy. Only the new faces – Roald and Katinka Høgmo – were unknown quantities.

They were also the ones who opened the proceedings, Katinka asked Ingrid if she was hungry, and Roald announced that they had assembled here to help her, Ingrid was ruining her life roaming around in the wilds like this, and that of her child, too. It sounded as if she were also ruining Roald Høgmo's life, and Ingrid realised the gathering must have been Hübner's work, Vollheim and his daughter had presumably driven here from Vollheim's farm during the night.

Mariann opened her mouth and repeated in a mumble what Høgmo had said.

Ingrid asked why she didn't look her in the eye when she spoke, she had also wanted to ask about this when they were at Vollheim farm, and she said so too.

Mariann didn't answer.

She was dressed differently from when they parted near Lake Kvarnberg, as though she had felt a need to smarten her appearance. The cardigan she had knitted for her father now hung over *his* shoulders, a worried man who kept fiddling with his wiry beard. Ingrid decided to accept the offer of food – and the next moment the admonitions swept across the table:

When a war's over, it's over, thank God, and should be forgotten, clocks move forwards, what has been lost cannot be retrieved . . . and time and time again they repeated that she ought to think about her child.

Ingrid was speechless.

Herman Vollheim said with a sheepish expression that the Russian people can hardly be called our allies anymore, but the British still are, he talked about Russia's catastrophic sufferings as well as fifteen million Europeans who still hadn't found their way home . . . refugees.

Ingrid had nothing to say to this, either.

"We have to learn to forget," he said.

"Eh?" Ingrid said, turning to Mariann, and telling her that she remembered her children's names, didn't she, she would never forget them, *would* she.

Mariann jumped to her feet and screamed that that had nothing to do with the matter, *none of them*, apart perhaps from Hübner, had the slightest idea what grief was like.

She didn't explain or elaborate why Hübner should have a better understanding of what grief was like than the rest of them, but the doctor clearly took this as encouragement and began to expatiate on the nature of grief, as he called it, the travails of reconciliation within the human psyche, making it all sound like both a gospel and an instruction manual.

Ingrid answered that she knew what grief was, it had nothing to do with this, her Alexander was alive.

"How do you know that?" Mariann shouted, then ran out of the room.

Ingrid watched her as she did so, felt a stab in the small of her back, stared from face to face and asked them if they were trying to lead her up the garden path, what was it they weren't telling her?

Høgmo quickly said, no, no, all he knew was that the Russian had left this place with one of the Resistance men who had offered to hide him on his farm.

"Hvar's that?" Ingrid said at once.

"Erm . . . near Røros."

"Hvar's that?"

The others exchanged glances, and Katinka asked why this Norwegian had risked his life for a Russian.

"He's a communist," Høgmo answered, annoyed by a question he deemed he had answered before, and added that he had lost touch with the man, he hadn't answered his letters.

Herman Vollheim let out a roar of scornful laughter. Ingrid turned to him and said:

"An' tha seid *A* war a clot?"

"Easy now, he's changed his mind about that," said Mariann, who had come in again. And this time she sat down on a chair next to Ingrid, so they were sitting shoulder to shoulder. "That's why he's here. You're . . ."

"Yes?" Ingrid said.

"Normal," Vollheim finished for her. "But there's something that doesn't add up . . ."

Ingrid asked what he was talking about.

In muted tones he tried to explain a disquiet he had felt when Ingrid arrived at his farm, but lost the thread, and the others stared in different directions, embarrassed.

Mariann leaned across the table and laid a hand on her father's, abruptly withdrew it again, got up and turned her back on them, but without leaving the room. Katinka got to her feet, too, and mumbled something about the *lefser* she had buttered, but she didn't leave the room either, and Hübner said that traumas are synonymous with an over-active memory, you think what you remember is true, but it isn't, it's a delusion, in here, he said, placing a finger against his temple.

Herman Vollheim asked irritably what that was supposed to mean.

Ingrid said there was a man missing here, someone called Nils, who had put her ashore in the middle of Lake Kvarnberg and made off with her ten Norwegian kroner.

Hübner asked who Nils was, and after a reluctant explanation from Mariann, said that he didn't know Nils, but his father had been a good man, hadn't he? And as for Nikolas . . .

"Ya, he isn't hier aither," Ingrid said.

"What do you mean?" Hübner said.

"A don't raitly know," Ingrid said with tears in her eyes.

Mariann said:

"What did I say!"

Hübner stood up and walked around the room gesticulating and muttering something that seemed to indicate his doubt that there had ever been a ship carrying Russian P.O.W.s that the British had bombed, causing a disaster on the scale of the *Titanic* . . .

Katinka asked what the *Titanic* was.

Roald whispered something in her ear that obviously offended her.

Hübner said none of them had ever heard of the *Rigel*, the

story wasn't plausible, whereupon he adopted a sombre expression and asked whether Ingrid hadn't set out on this journey owing to some misapprehension?

"No, no, the Russian does exist," Høgmo broke in crossly.

"How do you know? Can you speak Russian?"

Høgmo brushed Hübner's objection aside, and Katinka said, wait, and went into the kitchen, leaving an electric silence that lasted until she came back with a tray and began to put cups on the table.

Ingrid grabbed a *lefse*, broke off some for Kaja and asked the doctor why he had come all the way to Nordli to say only this, which he could have said yesterday.

Hübner sighed, and said that Ingrid had begun to interest him, the way she was walking around looking for something that didn't exist.

"Alexander *is* alive!" Ingrid said.

"And *she's* pretty too," Mariann said drily, looking at Hübner.

He rolled his eyes and said nothing.

Ingrid continued chewing, got up and asked Katinka if she could find some milk for Kaja. Katinka said, yes, of course, and Ingrid asked what this man was called, the one who had said he was willing to hide Alexander on his farm in Røros.

Nobody answered.

She repeated the question, which clearly embarrassed Katinka as she walked around the room showing Kaja the extensive collection of the Høgmo clan's historical mementos. Ingrid noticed that there were flowers in the window here too, in blue and grey pots, the kind they kept butter in on Barrøy. She asked if this was customary in both Sweden and Norway.

Katinka said the flowers had to be watered and ought to be outside, but Roald thought they were nicer inside the house.

Hübner asked what the hell they were talking about *now*.

Unruffled, Roald Høgmo turned to the flowers and said that his mother had liked them on the window sills and, in the same breath, mentioned a Resistance man he had written several letters to, a difficult character, who had been a partisan in Finnmark, and Ingrid made a note of his name.

"But the Russian was a good man," he added meditatively. "*He* didn't complain."

"No, and he had good table manners," Katinka said.

"He liked waffles," Høgmo added with a faraway smile.

"He liked everything," Katinka said.

"All three of them did," Høgmo added, and Herman Vollheim asked him crustily if he was sorry the war was over, why else would he have that stupid grin on his face?

"No, no, of course not. Are you crazy?" Høgmo retorted, whereafter Herman Vollheim told Ingrid in a grave voice that she should not trust this partisan, then turned to Høgmo without missing a beat and shouted in an accusatory tone:

"You just wanted to get rid of them!"

"Rubbish!" Høgmo shouted back.

"And which way did they go?"

117

Høgmo looked imploringly at his wife.

"South, along the border . . . ?" Katinka ventured.

"And why not straight into Sweden?"

Høgmo looked dejected.

"I don't know."

"Oh yes, you do!"

"Pappa, please!" Mariann said.

"And *how* did they go?"

"On skis."

"Could the Russian ski!?"

"We trained him at night. He became good at it."

Katinka confirmed this with a nod, and Høgmo eyed her with disdain. She recoiled, handed Kaja back to Ingrid and disappeared out of the door.

"It's a hundred kilometres to the next border crossing," Herman Vollheim persisted.

"Pappa!" Mariann said again.

"There are cabins," Høgmo said defiantly.

"Don't be so stupid. You sent them to a certain death."

"No!" Høgmo said.

"And the third man in the group, what did you two do with him?"

Høgmo cast a tormented glance at Hübner, who collected himself and said in Swedish:

"Yes, er, the fellow came over to us, didn't he . . . ?"

Nobody answered, or reacted, and Herman Vollheim's energy

was spent. He got to his feet, walked over to the window and stared out, above the flowers in the blue pot, with Mariann's steely gaze on his back. Ingrid whispered:

"An' thas knew this all th' taim?"

"No," Mariann said.

"Oh, shut up," Herman said to the windowpane.

"They might've made it," Mariann said with tears in her eyes.

"Oh, shut up," Herman said again. 'It was certain death, that's why you never got any replies to your letters, Roald. They'll be lying somewhere up in the mountains, what's left of them."

Mariann shuddered and sobbed openly. Ingrid looked at her in surprise, got up and opened the kitchen door and asked in a loud voice if she could wash some nappies there. Katinka said, yes, yes, and came and took her by the hand, like a redeeming angel, and led her out of the house and across a lawn that was almost as closely cropped as the one in the cemetery in Sweden, while Ingrid wondered what had come over Mariann, and it occurred to her that she would have to remember this, every expression, every word, every sound, like those symbols in a book she still wasn't able to read.

They entered what Katinka called the bathhouse, a white-washed brick building that stood next to a smallish tarred house, the retirement cottage where Roald Høgmo's parents had lived, Ingrid learned from Katinka, who was talking non-stop. There was a sink, and a wooden washboard, a glass and an aluminium washboard, hanging like paintings on the wall above a wash-boiler full of hot water. Katinka held Kaja while Ingrid did the washing, and amid her excited babble said that Ingrid shouldn't listen to what the menfolk said.

Ingrid asked her why not.

Katinka appeared to consider this a superfluous question.

Ingrid asked if she thought Kaja looked like the Russian.

"Yes," Katinka said, there was something about her eyes that made you recognise them whether you had seen them before or not.

Ingrid asked uneasily what she meant, and Katinka explained that, in her mind's eye, she could still see her own daughter out there on the grass, more clearly than she could see the other children, and it hadn't been like that before.

"Afore hva?"

Before the war. As though the war had also changed what happened *before* it. Ingrid heard the flapping of birds' wings, and felt the mutilated Russian hands on her hips and back and arms, smelled the sea in the steam from the sink, the nettles, the seaweed, the marshland . . . while snatches of the excruciating scene in the main house rang in her ears. She asked Katinka whether Alexander had been able to hold a pair of ski sticks?

Katinka nodded eagerly, put Kaja down on the ironing board and demonstrated how she had strapped his hands to the sticks, he used two sets of straps, and he was strong. He was also young, she added, making it sound as though he was far too young for

Ingrid.

She picked up Kaja again and laughed as though it were her own child, or as though all children were hers, and Ingrid heard her say that she could give her some of her savings to enable her to continue her journey, she could also make some food to take along.

"So *tha* doesn't think they'r deed?"

"No," Katinka said, that was what she meant when she said Ingrid shouldn't listen to the menfolk.

Ingrid asked if she had been up in the mountains a lot in the winter.

Katinka didn't answer. And Ingrid asked whether she could stay the night there, preferably without having to talk to anyone. Katinka said she understood, she looked almost relieved, and Høgmo's parents' house was empty, the sun was shining now too, so her washing would dry. They heard a car starting outside, Hübner's, a sound that first came closer, then faded in the distance and disappeared. Ingrid slumped down onto a chair carved out of a tree trunk and sat there, stock-still, until Katinka asked if there was something wrong.

"No," Ingrid said.

She felt dirty, from all this water that does not wash clean.

18

Herman Vollheim's watch showed it was no later than four in the morning when Ingrid Marie Barrøy got up in the cottage on Høgmo farm, with flames on her retinas, sand in her mouth, and still hearing the deafening voices of Hübner, and Høgmo and Vollheim.

She dressed silently, didn't eat, and tiptoed out of the house with the rucksack on her back and Kaja asleep on her belly – and walked straight into Mariann Vollheim, who was standing barefoot and large in the dew-covered grass, wearing a light summer dress that Ingrid hadn't seen before, a grey parcel pressed to her stomach, and barring her way.

Ingrid said she had expected to see her father.

Mariann said that if it had been up to him, then ... well.

Handed her the parcel and said it was a dress, so Ingrid wouldn't have to look like a tramp when she arrived home, because she was going home, wasn't she?

"Yes."

Mariann offered to drive her.

Ingrid saw the freckles on her neck, and reflected once again that she was a beautiful woman who would never know she was. She said she didn't want to be driven anywhere, neither by her nor her father, she would walk, and Mariann stood there, as usual looking elsewhere.

Ingrid asked if she wanted Herman's watch back.

"You must be joking."

Mariann stroked Kaja's nose with a finger, taking care not to wake her.

Ingrid asked what was so problematic about this man who had taken Alexander along with him.

Mariann said, with reluctance, that both the Rinnan gang and German agents had infiltrated their lines, so it was wise to mistrust more people than you trusted, but this could become a habit that was difficult to drop.

Ingrid said she understood.

Mariann said she doubted it, and that mistrust could develop into a problem which the Germans also knew how to exploit.

"A see," Ingrid mumbled, and added, probingly, that Hübner probably believed her Alexander existed, but not that he was Russian and from the *Rigel*, he believed he was a German – doesn't tha think?

Mariann nodded slowly.

"Does he believe Nikolas?" Ingrid went on.

"I suppose so."

Ingrid said something she hoped would be the last thing she said, which was that not everyone had been like Mariann and her father, she had been accompanied by a man with a large dog at the beginning of her journey, he seemed to support himself on it when he rested.

Mariann said that now she was scaring her.

Ingrid told her he was the only person to have said straight out that Alexander was dead and that it wasn't possible to cross the mountains in winter, and he had been wrong.

"Oh, yes?" Mariann said. "But these mountains are bigger."

Ingrid asked if she, too, believed they had perished.

Mariann looked down and muttered, yes, but added that she couldn't be sure, all she knew was that Alexander had left the farm here together with that savage, and no-one had heard from them since.

Ingrid had another question, about the man who died on the way from Lake Tunnsjø to here, how did that happen?

"I don't know," Mariann said.

Ingrid Marie Barrøy thanked her, and without another word walked out of the farmyard carrying Kaja on her belly, the rucksack on her back and the dress under her arm, down a dry, dirt-road that was covered with sparkling drops of dew, turned west and didn't look back, and heard no shouts or protests. A bird screeched in the silence. The sun met her face on the first hill. She gazed down across rolling, forest-clad landscape and a lake that lay as lifeless and flat as a grey stone floor.

When the eyes she felt on her back were gone, she climbed up a forest service track, sat down on a tree stump and cried until she saw by Herman Vollheim's watch that sixteen minutes had passed. The voices had fallen silent. The images lay stacked on top of one another. The details. The symbols. She had looked at the map and knew where she was. She held Kaja up to her face, got to her feet and went back to the road, and it felt like a relief that the bag Katinka had packed was heavy.

19

The rivers and streams of the Scandinavian peninsula run downwards from the backbone between the countries of Norway and Sweden, forming a crooked fishbone pattern. Ingrid walked down, following the Norwegian river Sanddøla, a distant and bottle-green rush of water, past the roots of a rugged spruce forest which resembled the teeth of a saw on the precipitous mountainsides. Through this same valley ran a road with so many bends that it was hardly worthy of the name. Ingrid took cover every time she heard the purr of an engine and ventured back onto the gravel as soon as it was quiet again. She counted six cars and two empty buses, and was caught up by a horse-drawn cart with an old, stooped man, who shouted that there was no point offering the lady a lift, he was just going down to the field over there. As he passed by, Ingrid wished him a pleasant day. And the horse was walking at such a leisurely pace and disappeared so slowly that she didn't feel she was being left behind.

There were so few birds that she was able to turn to look at each one, and none of them was a seagull or a tern or a cormorant, she was walking through a realm of silence. There were flies and midges and clegs and dust and pollen beneath clouds so feather-light that they can only float above dry land. The journey's own momentum returned to her legs – she walked and rested and walked until she turned off the road and slumped down on a patch of grass where nobody had ever sat before. She asked Kaja if she was hungry, what she thought of the silence, whether she wanted to go home to Barrøy or find a father, questions it was vital to ask a child who couldn't answer – they had reached a magical stage of the journey, uncharted territory.

Ingrid walked for three more kilometres and then sat down beneath a spruce tree shaped like a tent, where likewise nobody had ever sat before, spread a woollen blanket over the ground and watched Kaja crawling, Katinka's food, milk, bread, sausage, smoked fish ... the jam jar that looked like a jewel, and Herman Vollheim's porcelain cup that didn't resemble anything at all. She took off her shoes and massaged her feet and rolled onto her back and blinked her eyes at the smell of road-dust and resin, held Kaja in the crook of her right arm and repeated that she would have to learn to walk, to run after her father, after the birds, the lambs, the calves.

Kaja laughed and lay down beside her, staring up at the spruce needles until her eyelids drooped shut. Now Ingrid could sleep, too, without dreaming. She was woken by the chilly air, and spread the other blanket over them. The sun hung low in the north-west, the insects had fallen silent, the river was closer now, she went back to sleep and had no dreams.

Kaja and the rucksack weighed roughly the same, so Ingrid walked with a straight back, fifteen kilos heavier than she normally was, and had to keep taking rests over the sixty-nine kilometres to the next milestone, the fabled railway her own father had helped to build when there was poverty on the islands.

Like every wanderer, she made the discovery that those who come to a place first, and settle there, are more apprehensive than those who follow after them, as they have built something they are fearful of losing again. However, Ingrid was also a woman, and moreover she was carrying this child on her belly. So she was given milk at one farm and bread at another. One smallholding projected so far into the road that she had to cross the farmyard. An extremely old man came out and said:

"What are you doing?"

"A'm walken," Ingrid said.

"Where to?"

Then she also had to tell her story to someone it didn't concern, a blind man, who in addition wanted to give her a present, a knife that was hardly distinguishable from the one Carl had found under the tree root in the Kongsfjordfjell mountains.

But Ingrid had the knife she needed; she had her father's.

"Wait, wait," he said, and pulled her into a dark, tiny sitting room, where his aged wife lay in a bed that was as wide as it was long, staring up at them with small, bright eyes, as though she was searching for life, and stretched out a hard, wrinkled hand.

There was no need for Ingrid to tell her who she was or why she was there, she just held this cold tree-root of a human hand, and showed her Kaja, who smiled at the old woman, who smiled back, revealing toothless gums. Then Ingrid set off again on the same winding road and slept beneath another tent-like spruce tree.

She got up as usual, purged of sleep and travel-weariness, and covered the final kilometres with the dust swirling around her bartered miner's shoes, and reached the railway, which at this very place – in Formofoss – wends its way past a red station building with logs stacked against its south wall.

And once again reality descends upon her journey.

For the railway admits of no doubt and no compromises, it runs either north or south and all it has to offer her is the impossible dilemma of travelling home again having achieved nothing or continuing in the bewildering battlefield of peace-time, driven by a hope that is barely alive after the bedlam at Høgmo farm.

Yet her defiance is still intact, Ingrid's defiance is born of the sea in the face of all these people who wish her so well, or themselves, it is difficult to say, defiance is a small, hard ball of fury wrapped in woolly thoughts, the only question is whether this is enough.

*

Next to the wood pile stood a bench. On it sat a man in uniform, sleeping in the sun, his arms locked across his chest, his weather-beaten head resting against his right shoulder, saliva dribbling from the corner of his mouth, and Ingrid could smell alcohol.

He opened first one eye, then the other, and jumped up thinking he couldn't wipe the sleep from his face in a sufficiently dignified manner, he cast a glance at the clock on the wall, and Ingrid asked if the train went to Røros. He mumbled, yes, but, well, no, and suddenly appeared to recognise her, she would have to change at Trondheim, an insurmountable obstacle.

"A see," Ingrid said.

He asked if she was sure she knew where she was going, and Ingrid narrowed her eyes at yet another instance of unhelpfulness, spotted a post horn next to the sign showing that Formofoss was 64 metres above sea level, and asked if he too had a telephone.

"Yes, we do. And telegraph."

She asked if anyone had phoned him recently.

He looked perplexed.

Ingrid sat down on the bench and removed the shawl from around Kaja and asked if he knew anyone in Nordli.

"Yes," he said without any hesitation, then seemed to regret this and repeated his question as to whether she was sure she wanted to go to Røros.

"Hva does th' ticket cost?" Ingrid said.

He said he would have to go and find out, nobody goes to Røros, but didn't move, shuffled his feet, and said it would be a long time before the train came, and the northbound one would be coming first, wouldn't she rather take that?

Ingrid smiled and asked him what his name was.

It was Hans Kvåle.

Ingrid said her name was Ingrid, and he gave up.

"I don't want anything to do with this," he said. A door opened and slammed shut again. By now Ingrid had also given up, or found a way forward, this wasn't quite clear yet, but it soon would be.

20

The railway was built on foundations of political sorcery and indomitable will, on the basis of planned national aspirations, arrogance and terror; it required exorbitant sums of money and inhuman toil through peace and war and peace again. It was built on thousands of broken Norwegian backs, and the same number of Russian and Yugoslavian dead, and is called Blood Road, because that is what it is. And the north-bound train that approaches can be heard from a greater distance than the human eye can see, like a hissing, snarling ice-drift on the horizon, it is accompanied by blasts of a horn and flashing lights and more clatter than there is room for between the mountain slopes on either side, as it thunders in and groans to a halt, spewing smoke and sparks.

By now the station is no longer deserted but populated by muttering men and women and children, who individually or in groups have arrived on foot, in cars, or on carts or bicycles, a freshly scrubbed and humble gathering, who stand sweating in the dazzling sunshine and look as though they are waiting for the life-changing arrival of a steamship.

An elderly man gets off the train, a cloth cap on his head and a knapsack on his back. Nobody greets or embraces him. A mother and a boy follow, they, too, in their Sunday best, and are surrounded by a crowd of old and young, who keep their welcome as muted and restrained as possible, as though ashamed of it.

And only one person gets on, a gentleman in a black suit, who, on the top step, doffs his hat and waves it a single time, although no-one takes any notice. He disappears through the door at the end of the carriage. And the stationmaster, Hans Kvåle, exchanges a few parting words with his mobile colleague, who is standing on the lowest footboard of the last carriage, waving a green flag, so the monster can snort into action again and haul its coaches into the distance, this departing rumble of thunder that is of much shorter duration than the roar of the train's arrival. Afterwards, the people shuffle homewards in the same mumbling, piecemeal manner in which they arrived, leaving Ingrid to sit alone once more in silence on the bench next to the pile of logs, reflecting on the fact that she didn't take the northbound train, that this is how it should be, it couldn't have been otherwise.

She hears the crunch of footsteps on gravel, and Hans Kvåle comes up and stands in front of her. He says:

"So you're still here, are you?"

And repeats: "I don't want to have anything to do with this."

But he hands her two small pieces of cardboard, which turn out to be one ticket to Trondheim and one ticket from Trondheim to Røros, the child travels free. He mumbles the price and goes in again before Ingrid can get out her money, she is unsure whether she heard him say that the train would not be arriving until the middle of the night, and she knows she ought to have a wash.

She opens the parcel she got from Mariann when they parted in Nordli and holds up a green and white flowery dress, which she doesn't need to try on, it fits. She stands up and goes into the waiting room and pays for the tickets and asks Hans Kvåle through a hole in a glass hatch whether there is running water in his lavatory over there. He answers yes, twice, as though to reassure himself, and she notices a half-full bottle of clear spirits on his writing desk, beside a large glass, which is almost empty.

21

When Ingrid Marie Barrøy got on the train at Formofoss railway station in a new dress a little before three o'clock in the morning, the stationmaster, Hans Kvåle, had confessed to her that for safety's sake he had been on both sides in the war. He hadn't had anything against anyone. Nonetheless, he had been a guard at this P.O.W. camp in Botn, Nordland, because his family needed money, but he shouldn't have done that, because it wasn't easily forgotten. He had told her about his three sons, who had attended different schools in three different towns in southern Norway, as though they were in hiding, while his wife lived in Gjøvik with their eight-year-old daughter.

He had also divulged that it had been a deliberate punishment on the part of the state railways to post him to this godforsaken hole, and it was of no consolation that the station had living quarters and electricity and mains water, both hot and cold, when there was nobody else living here apart from himself, one man with four rooms and a kitchen, and that dispiriting spruce forest, no matter which window he might choose to look out of, it was a joke, he said, in a dialect which during the night increasingly came to resemble Suzanne's when she arrived on Barrøy in the last year of the war, from Oslo.

Hans Kvåle had also touched Ingrid's knee with his right hand on three occasions, and she had pushed it away an equal number of times. He had asked if she wanted to borrow a sleeping bag, a bed, a blanket, he had knocked back a whole bottle of spirits, fallen asleep twice, woken up twice, and said six times that Ingrid ought to go back home post bloody haste, not that it was anything to do with him, she would never find what she was looking for.

In addition, he had lit the round stove in the waiting room, and given her a large pillow with a navy-blue pillowcase, which she could put on the bench like a buffer between them and use as a bed for Kaja. When the clock finally turned three and the southbound train arrived with the same swaggering and earth-shaking racket as its northbound counterpart, he carried Ingrid's sleeping child on board and into an empty compartment, let Ingrid keep the pillow and gave her back the money for the ticket in addition to five kroner from his own pocket, without looking at her, and without any words of farewell except:

"Sorry."

He scurried out again and waved the green flag in the white darkness, and that was the last Ingrid Marie Barrøy saw of Hans Kvåle. And as not even *he* is a credible witness, or a principled man one can trust, or someone who sees it in his interest for the truth to come to light, or someone who has distinguished himself in a way anyone cares to remember – in fact, he does his very best to erase himself from everyone's memory – it is of no consequence that his personal details are recorded in Ingrid's sketch pad, on one of the last four pages, after the section where she tries to describe the swarms of midges in Sanddøla valley and Kaja's many bites, because Ingrid would never dream of disclosing any of this information.

She sat still on a cold seat of stiff, brown leather, listening to the clickety-clack of wheels on the rails and smelled iron and rock and forest and creosote, an inland smell on an inland night. She counted two more stations, where nobody got either on or off, and a third, where a largish group of people came on board and sat down in the next compartment, at which time Herman Vollheim's watch showed twenty to five.

A conductor came and punched a hole in one of her tickets, said that they were on schedule for the connecting train to Røros, smiled down at Kaja, who was asleep on Hans Kvåle's blue pillow, and went into the adjoining compartment where he told the people to quieten down; there was a child sleeping next door, Ingrid heard him bawl over the hubbub before the sliding door slammed shut and the sun formed a golden triangle on the middle seat opposite her.

Her eyelids closed.

And she reflected that if Alexander had survived the journey across the mountains from Kongsmoen to Skorovas, then he could well have survived another range of mountains, however immense it was, for some strange reason all this seemed clearer to her now, sitting here in the train after the decision had been taken, than when she left Høgmo farm and Mariann Vollheim's incredulous face.

For the last few hours as they approached the town, Ingrid shared the compartment with two young soldiers in uniform and a middle-aged woman, and she had a strong sense that all three of them were staring strangely at her.

She wondered if it was because she smelled, but all that met her nostrils when she wiped the back of her hand across her face was Hans Kvåle's station soap. She did her best to look out of the window, where in the reflection she saw the eyes of one of the soldiers move away. The woman sitting directly opposite her, her plump knees pressed together, was knitting a small sweater and announced without warning, into her lap – as though to everyone present – that it was for her youngest grand-child, whom she was going to visit in Trondheim and hadn't seen since Christmas.

Ingrid gave a start, as though she had been caught red-handed watching her, and said that the sweater was very nice, but the pattern looked complicated. The woman held the knit-ting aloft to inspect it, and said, no, it wasn't, still without looking at Ingrid, then carried on knitting and suddenly muttered that Ingrid should stop staring at her.

"A'm counten," Ingrid said.

"What?"

"A count ev'rythin'."

She looked out of the window, where the soldier's gaze once again evaded hers, and from there down at Kaja, who was still asleep, placed a hand under her head, and the woman said it was a pretty child, did Ingrid have any others?

"No."

"I've got five."

One of the soldiers got to his feet and manoeuvred his way between two sets of women's knees and leaned against the window.

"Stjørdal," said the woman with the knitting, without looking up.

He thanked her and sat down again, and Ingrid began to sweat, sniffed the back of her hand once more and was considering waking Kaja when the other soldier let out a stifled groan and got up and went into the corridor, while his companion stared straight at the floor as though he were taking an oral exam he had no chance of passing.

The woman with the knitting said that maybe they should have a drop of hot milk, and pulled out a shiny steel Thermos flask, put two cups on a small folding table that she raised into position between them, and when their eyes met above the steaming milk Ingrid repeated that she only had one child, Kaja.

"Yes, you said that," the woman answered and began to

question her about where she came from and where she was going. Ingrid sat with her hands in her lap and replied politely that she didn't feel like speaking. The woman asked if she was unhappy about something. Ingrid stared straight ahead and said she wanted to go home, the train was going in the wrong direction.

The woman screwed up her eyes and placed a hand on Ingrid's knee. The other soldier also got up and went out. The woman pulled down the roller blind over the glass pane in the door. Ingrid leaned forwards and put her face in her hands and wept until eventually she was able to distinguish one sob from another, wiped her cheeks with her fingers and made no attempt to explain her outburst, she had no idea what was going on.

The woman drank some hot milk. Ingrid looked out of the dirty window and asked how old her grandchild was, the one the sweater was for.

"Two."

Ingrid asked how many grandchildren she had.

"Twelve."

Ingrid smiled and asked her if she could teach her how to knit with two strands of wool – that pattern there.

The woman asked whether Ingrid wouldn't prefer to lie down on the bench seat and get a little shuteye, she looked worn out. Ingrid said that she was never worn out. The woman chuckled noiselessly, shrugged, and said that Ingrid's milk was getting cold. Ingrid drank some lukewarm milk, said yes to

more, and both watched and listened as the woman demonstrated knitting patterns and techniques. She was also allowed
to try her hand at a few rows herself, was corrected whenever
she made a mistake, and understood everything the stranger
said. One of the soldiers came back in, pulled a monster of a
kitbag down from the luggage rack, said sorry, and disappeared
for good.

22

Ingrid Marie Barrøy got off the train in Trondheim having made two firm resolutions: to stay awake, and *not* to leave the station, the very notion of a town was overwhelming. She found a vacant bench inside a spacious, high-ceilinged waiting room with more sound and echoes than the sea, and more people than in the whole of Skorovas on a Saturday afternoon. And sat gazing at Kaja's face, she was awake and had eaten and was looking around with an unearthly serenity in those Russian eyes of hers.

A young man leaned over them and asked loudly if Ingrid wanted to buy a newspaper.

She answered "no" in a voice that was as quiet as his was loud, and caught sight of the woman from the compartment, who was talking to a man in uniform. He turned to face the bench, listened to something the woman was whispering in his ear, and began to move towards her, with the woman hard on his heels. He stopped and asked if everything was all right, could Ingrid identify herself, where had she come from and where was she going, four questions and a short pause between each.

Ingrid didn't answer any of them.

"Stand up, would you, please."

Ingrid stood up, and he asked if she was feeling all right.

"Yes," Ingrid said.

"You're trembling," the man said.

"No," Ingrid said, taking an unsteady step to one side. He took her arm and helped her to sit down again, and asked, without any edge to his voice, if she had eaten.

Ingrid nodded and felt the flapping of wings on her skin, but also a sensation that was beginning to resemble nausea, a stench. And heard a voice saying that this journey wasn't real, it was a dream which couldn't end well, even were she to have the good fortune to awaken, it was impossible to wake up.

But she managed to draw a breath, and said, ignoring the man in uniform and the woman from the compartment, that she had recently received news of someone's death, a close member of her family, one of her sisters was dead.

She wiped her eyes with the back of her hand, gazed at Kaja, who was looking up at her in puzzlement, and held her daughter under the arms so that she could stand on her lap and try to balance on wobbly legs. Ingrid laughed, and said soon she would be able to walk. They were going to visit family in Røros, she said without looking up, did the man know when the train departed?

He frowned and turned to look at a large information board hanging above the doors leading to the platforms, a board with train times Ingrid knew off by heart, and said that the train would be leaving in half an hour. But then he just stood there, and murmured that Ingrid should take care, she was in a town now.

Ingrid acknowledged this fact with a nod, though it was impossible to comprehend its full implications, and then he too nodded, and left.

But the stench and nausea remained. Ingrid shouted into the crowd, he reappeared and stared at her quizzically. She shouted, "Thanks," and waved to him with Kaja's hand.

He touched his cap in a stiff salute, then was gone for ever. Ingrid scanned the room, looking for the woman from the compartment, but she had gone, too. And she felt that she was beginning to regain her equilibrium, which in the course of the hours on the train had left her so gradually that she hadn't noticed.

Then she began to wonder whether she had met the uniformed man before, whether she had seen the woman in the compartment before, whether she knew Hans Kvåle from a previous time. Mariann and her father? Hübner . . . ?

But they also disappeared from her mind, one face at a time. She took out her sketch pad, ignored the drawings from her childhood this time as well, jotted down the train times and a record of an old man who wanted to give her a knife, his bedridden wife in a poverty-stricken house, as well as the name she ought to have noted earlier at Høgmo farm, that of a partisan from Finnmark, but she had no difficulty remembering it.

23

On the next train, Ingrid sat in an open coach, as on a bus, together with thirteen other passengers all staring in the same direction without saying a word to one another. She looked out upon another valley and a river that resembled the Sand-døla, terrain with spruce and then pine forests, which gradually decreased in height and eventually disappeared altogether, such that the train could rumble through open summer landscapes, mountains far in the distance, a close copy of the countryside Alexander and then she herself had walked through from the sea to Skorovas, she following in his tracks, in the summer, which he had left in the winter, and she said aloud that he had been *here*, too, in this train, she could feel it, and fell silent, ashamed, when the man in the seat in front turned and sent her an alarmed glance over his shoulder.

She had something to eat, and fed Kaja, still using Katinka's provisions. They finished the jar of jam and drank water from a container that stood in a metal cage-like contraption near the door, which Ingrid had seen the other passengers helping themselves to. Another conductor came past and punched a hole in the second of her tickets. Outside the window the river was getting wider and wider, and the train trundled into a station where four of the thirteen passengers alighted. Ingrid leaned forwards to ask the man in the seat in front a question, but he had already half-turned and said:

"You have to get off at the next stop."

Ingrid asked how on earth he could have known that.

Facing the train window, he answered that he couldn't help but overhear her conversation with the conductor.

"And the next station is Røros."

Ingrid apologised and let Kaja crawl down to the floor and play with a newspaper that had been left behind. She closed her eyes and didn't open them again as long as she could hear the rustling of paper and the sound of it being torn to pieces. Now the train had begun to brake again. And she sensed that he had been *here* before, too. But also reflected that she couldn't trust herself anymore, and thought about all the things she didn't understand and how the journey had drained her of energy in a way she had never before experienced.

Ingrid Marie Barrøy got off the train at Røros and walked into the station and asked a uniformed, though far younger, colleague of Hans Kvåle's – who was also sitting behind a glass hatch with a circular hole to speak through, the sign said – whether he knew anyone in town by the name of Arne Moen Juvet, she read it aloud from her pad, information provided by Roald Høgmo.

"No, not from these parts."

Ingrid looked at him.

"Hva's not fr'm these parts ... ?"

"The name."

"Ar tha sure?"

He sent her a faraway look.

Ingrid walked out again, and began to go from door to door in the streets closest to the station, from shop to shop, asked the same question at a hotel reception desk, stopped a nun in the street and went into a cobbler's, he too said that Juvet was not a local name.

When evening fell, she went into a cemetery above the town and sought shelter behind the stone wall, where she sank into a deep sleep with Kaja on her belly.

Ingrid's dream: the voice came from behind her, but she didn't turn round. Barrøy was both white and green, it was both winter and summer, and beside her, where the ground slopes down to the sea in the south, sat Alexander, dressed as though he had always lived there, not in her father's clothes, which Ingrid had given him during the war, but in his own. He sat with his elbows resting on his knees and his eyes examining his undamaged fingers. He didn't look at her as he talked – about the hay and the snow and a chain of nets they had lost in the sea ... There was a short distance between them, but it wasn't noticeable. Ingrid smiled at his profile, and responded to him in the same everyday tone. And when he began speaking again, it struck her that she could pick every word out of his mouth, like pebbles, and weigh them in her hands, because he spoke her language, and she spoke his. This was the first image, and she didn't turn round.

In the second, Kaja was sitting in front of them playing in the heather with something they couldn't see, a net float, a gull's egg, a conch . . . something that was smaller than her white hands. Nor was it possible to see how old she was, whether she could get to her feet and stand, whether she could walk, run, for she was sitting with her back to them, in deep concentration. But Ingrid noticed that Alexander and herself were the same age, and she felt that this was good.

In the third image, he was lying with his head in her lap, his eyes closed. But he wasn't asleep, and she understood every word he said; then she caught sight of the plait hanging down across her field of vision, dangling above his face – she saw that the plaited hair was white, while the wool braid binding it together was red or green or black. In this image, they were alone. They were old. It was complete, and she didn't turn round.

The sun had dried the dew on half of the blanket. Ingrid wriggled into the sunshine and sat with her back against the wall and could see the heads of people walking past in the street outside the cemetery, a street in the town of Røros, they looked as if they were on their way to work, the same work at the same time, and there was no more bread left.

But Ingrid was strangely untroubled as she packed, though this unaccustomed feeling didn't have any real impact until she found herself in a bakery – where here, too, she enquired in vain about Juvet – and was suddenly forced to admit to herself that this man didn't exist, he had never existed.

She had *sensed* it yesterday, now she *knew*.

She was given the loaf, paid, and went out again light of foot and heart, down the main street of an enormous town, wondering why this didn't hurt, why she didn't feel the slightest twinge of disappointment at being on her way back home, having failed in her mission, at having given up, now she could also hear the cries of seagulls and the wind, an inner orchestra in the unnatural quietness that reigns in a living town.

She went into the railway station to buy a ticket, from the same official, who recognised her and asked if she had found the man she was looking for.

Ingrid said no, she was going north, but suddenly remembered the telephone directory she had seen at the hotel reception desk – the telephone and the railway, which connected all corners of the country – and asked if they also had one there at the station.

"Of course."

But he had already looked up the name, yesterday.

"Rielly?" Ingrid said.

"Yes, just after you'd gone. Just to check. And nobody . . . what was his name . . . ?"

"Can A have a keek?" Ingrid said.

He stood up with a wearied expression and disappeared into what was obviously a telegraph office and returned with a dog-eared directory. Ingrid could find no Arne Moen Juvet, neither under M nor J, and wondered why she was still doing this when she should be on her way home.

She looked up and her eyes met another uniformed, but far older, man leaning against the door frame and smoking a cigarette. He returned her gaze, disappeared into the back room and came back with a tattered notebook, which contained thirty or so handwritten names on every other page. A nicotine-stained finger ran down the page with the letter B on it and stopped below one of the names.

"Belteren . . . ?" Ingrid read, upside down.

"The man you're looking for doesn't have a telephone. He can be reached at this number, at Belteren farm, if anyone needs to get hold of him."

"Hvur does tha know that?" Ingrid asked.

The finger moved towards the spine of the book and over into the column on the opposite page, where there was the name A. M. Juvet, together with some symbols she couldn't decipher.

"Who wrote that?" his younger colleague asked.

"I did," said the man with the cigarette. "That's why I knew. I remembered it yesterday."

He went back into the telegraph office, fetched a map and spread it out on the table where Ingrid had placed Kaja and the rucksack, under the window looking out onto the platform. They leaned over. There was no sign of the farm.

Ingrid smiled.

"P'raps we can telephone?"

The man slapped his forehead and went back into the telegraph office again. Ingrid and the other official heard half of a short conversation, the older man came out and said pensively that they didn't know of any Juvet there, either.

"So?" his colleague said, vexed.

"He also said something I didn't understand. Then he hung up."

The older man came around the counter once more, leaned over the notebook and studied the symbols next to Juvet.

"Well, I ask you," his colleague chortled. "You wrote it yourself, and you can't read it."

"I wrote the *name*, not the symbols. They have something to do with the war. And unless I'm very much mistaken, I noted down the name two or maybe three years ago. That's how we did it. But it wasn't me who added the symbols."

They began to discuss the shifting county borders and staff who had worked at the station, mentioned names and rejected them again, when the man with the cigarette appeared to come up with another idea, went around the counter and stuck his yellow finger under a barely legible name next to a tiny square symbol.

"Belteren farm."

"Yes?" Ingrid said.

"They were one of the first to get a telephone."

This, too, clearly set his mind working. "I can see by the number," he explained. And Ingrid asked how she could get there, to this valley where Belteren farm was. He said:

"By train. And bus."

But corrected this to: "Or rather two buses. And then you have to go the rest of the way on foot. It's quite a walk."

Ingrid nodded.

He went into the office to telephone, leaving his cigarette smoking in an ashtray, which was green and made of glass, like a net float, came back and announced that the first bus would be leaving in just over an hour, showed Ingrid on the map where she should change, and when she thanked him, he asked her if she had a map.

"Ya."

He asked to see it. Ingrid got out her maps, Adolf Malvika and Mariann Vollheim's. With a pen, he marked a cross where there was no name on Mariann's map and no square.

Ingrid folded it up and thanked him again. His colleague said, wasn't she going north?

Ingrid said no, thanked him, too, and walked out of the station with the same ease of mind that should have brought her home, and found the stop for a bus that would take her even further away, now also with a hint of excitement running through her. She found a wooden bin to sit on. Around her she smelled earth and forest and fields. She wondered whether to make a few more notes, about the staff at the station perhaps. But she hadn't got their names, hardly remembered their faces, and the sun was shining brighter than ever before.

Ingrid Marie Barrøy was in the middle of the country, a good 700 kilometres from home. She was sitting on a wooden bin filled with sand counting cars and bicycles and listening to engines and loud and soft voices, until counting also became one of the purposes of the journey. She counted prams and mothers and watched as a locomotive trundled past with an endless line of wagons carrying timber. She watched three small boys running around in a mixture of dirt and sawdust, kicking a heavy, brown ball which reached up to the middle of their thin, bare calves. And when she spotted the bus, she was on the verge of counting that, too. And it occurred to her that over the past half hour or so she had forgotten everything, that she hadn't thought about where she was or whither she was going, she hadn't thought about Alexander or her father, her mother, Barbro . . . She clambered up the steps onto the bus and into the muggy smell of people enclosed in a ferocious heat, took a deep breath and found a seat which stuck to her thighs, held Kaja up to a narrow slatted window under the luggage rack, which she opened, and Ingrid heard her laugh and watched the wind playing in her hair as the bus moved off.

24

Ingrid Marie Barrøy was the only passenger to alight from the dusty bus at a desolate crossroads late in the afternoon, sweaty, drowsy and desperately tired. She walked five long kilometres through swarms of insects amidst rolling meadows and resplendent farms and had to get out her map and try to remember the railway clerk's hand movements as he marked the cross where Belteren farm was, it seemed to be situated between two roads, and she didn't know which of them she was on.

She passed a farm estate, where nobody was at home, and an ancient church, which was locked, and came upon a weather-beaten sign at a road junction, bearing letters which, with a measure of goodwill, could be construed as Belteren 1 km.

The road followed a stream up through a wooded glade and led her in between two fields beneath a honey sky. She espied six buildings, vast potato fields and brown-and-white cows grazing. And more and longer hay-drying racks than she had ever seen in her life.

A figure came out of the farmhouse, a young man, she could see by the way he moved, who was walking in the direction of the road to cut her off at the entrance to the drive, he must have seen her long before she saw him.

Once again Ingrid told her story, and, unmoved, the newcomer repeated – every time she took a breath – that she had come to the wrong place.

This farm is called Belteren, isn't it, she said.

"Yes."

There was a milk ramp by the driveway. Ingrid put down her rucksack, laid Kaja on a blanket and changed her. He stood watching. She waited for him to go back to the farmhouse. He didn't. She got out her sketch pad and showed him her own clear handwriting.

"No. No Juvet here."

She looked at him and he looked at her. Ingrid drew a deep breath and cast around, wrapped up Kaja again, secured her to her belly, and stood waiting, as though to give him one last chance, a young man in a flannel shirt and breeches and bare, brown calves ending in a pair of black clogs, handsome, clean-shaven, regular features, a man with his hands in his pockets and a steely expression in his large, grey eyes. But again – nothing can end in this manner.

Ingrid said she had walked a long way to get here.

That didn't make any impression on him, either.

She searched for something to say to break down this wall, but he beat her to it and said that if she really didn't believe him, she could go on up to the last farm, he pointed, and ask there, at Brynet, then she could leave here with not a doubt in her mind.

"Tha's odd," Ingrid said.

He shrugged.

Ingrid turned and began to walk back the same way, but stopped after twenty metres. He was still standing by the ramp, staring at her.

"Arn't tha goen back in?" she shouted.

He threw out an arm dismissively and made his way towards the farm, slowly. Ingrid waited until he had been swallowed up by the shadow of the farmhouse, took another spontaneous decision, walked back past the ramp and two or three hundred metres further up the slope, then turned and saw that he was still standing where the sun and shadows met, watching her. She carried on up in the evening light, which had turned an even deeper shade of honey.

Brynet farm lay on the south-facing hillside, in the crook of a dusty cart track that lost itself in the wide expanses, surrounded by a birch forest and vast fields with unbounded views to the south and east, bluish-black wooded mountainsides, a dry, silent desert, it was now late evening.

The farmhouse was made from tarred timber, with blue carvings on the frames and barge-boards, and had two matching front doors, each beneath its own porch, it resembled two houses in one. A black weathervane stood still on one of the rooftops.

Ingrid could not hear any animals, she saw none either, but the fields had been mown, and half of the hay-racks wound their way like empty fences down towards a shallow valley, where, in brief glimpses, she could make out a glittering stream.

She heard the sounds of an axe and walked round to the back of the house, spotted a man who was chopping wood in the last rays of the sun, with his back to her. He stiffened, but carried on. She called out, he slowly turned and stood there peering at her, caught sight of Kaja, lodged his axe in the chopping block and strode over to them.

"Let's have a peek at the kid."

Ingrid held Kaja up for him to see. He studied her, running a hand down his cheek, it was covered with a black leather glove which extended up over a powerful forearm with prominent blue veins and three white scars around the elbow.

"Well, well."

Ingrid was at a loss to know what to say. "Well, well," he repeated, and switched his gaze to Ingrid. "So you do exist, after all."

Ingrid essayed a smile.

He was dressed in dungarees and a checked shirt, like a farmer, and was wearing large, brown boots, though he gave more the impression of being a doctor or a priest, a clean-shaven man in his forties, with bristly, grizzled hair and clear, brown eyes, which looked right through her, Ingrid felt, with a shudder. A tiny pump was pulsating beneath the skin of his left cheek, and Ingrid had to look away.

"Come inside," he said, grabbing her rucksack and beginning to walk. He turned when she didn't react, and arched his eyebrows.

Ingrid followed him into a large kitchen, even more sumptuous than the living room at Høgmo farm, the windows were tall, and the view expansive. He didn't invite her to sit down, but asked how she had found him, as though this question couldn't have been asked outside in the farmyard. Ingrid mentioned the unhelpful man at Belteren, the farm she could now just make out through one of the windows, the highest-lying group of buildings in a community which meandered downwards level by level and vanished into a blue haze.

"Bernhard," he nodded. "And before him?"

Ingrid told him her story, and felt that it still lacked something, but he understood everything she said and nodded at every piece of the puzzle that fell into place, as though she were being tested on her homework, which he knew more about than her, and when she mentioned the symbols in the notebook at Røros station he almost smiled, and said that his name was neither Moen nor Juvet, but anyone who wanted to get in touch with him had to omit the Moen part when they rang Bernhard.

Ingrid said:

"Hva?"

He shrugged and said it was an arrangement they had from the war days, he didn't like visitors, no doubt they had told her that.

"Hvo?"

"The people in Nordli. It must've been Roald Høgmo who sent you here, wasn't it, or the folk at Vollheim?"

"The' think tha's deed," Ingrid said.

"And a good job, too," he said, and set about slicing a freshly baked loaf on the worktop next to the window. Neither he nor Ingrid said anything as the knife cut through the bread. Ingrid counted the slices and was unable to utter her fateful question: whether Alexander was alive or not and what he might have said about her, if, that is, the two of them had been able to communicate at all.

She held Kaja by the hands and let her toddle about on the floor. He cast sidelong glances at them, and asked how things were with Herman and Mariann, whether *she* had any children, too.

Ingrid said they had died.

"Oh," he said. "How tragic."

He asked Ingrid if she would like a cup of tea. She said she had never tasted tea.

"It's about time, then."

Ingrid asked if he lived alone.

"Yes."

He said — once again to the breadboard — that he and his sister had inherited this farm from their mother, but he had grown up in Finnmark with his father, the family had done business with the Russians for several generations, out of Vardø and Kiberg. Ingrid said he didn't talk like someone from Finnmark.

He spoke a few words, it sounded as though he was singing, and Ingrid burst into laughter, controlled herself, and quietly mentioned that she knew some people in Skarsvåg.

"Skarsvåg was burned down," he said.

"They'r bilden it up," Ingrid countered.

He eyed her and said in his former dialect that he had been expecting her. And she asked if Alexander was alive.

"Yes, yes indeed."

Of course Alexander is alive. No-one could be more alive. But, for fear that she might have misheard, Ingrid quickly said that it was good to be here. And when he didn't reply, she told him frantically about her dizziness on the train, she had felt as if she were floating in water.

He said that was a strange expression to use, and asked how long she had been on the road. Ingrid totted up the days, and together with the two weeks in Skorovas, it came to maybe a month, and he said that being alone makes you go daft in the head, and, believe me, I know what I'm talking about.

"No," Ingrid laughed.

He eyed her once again.

She spotted a small toy car by the log bin and asked if Kaja could play with it. He said yes, please do. She asked whether he had any children. Yes, two, in Oslo, they were grown up now, but the car had belonged to his sister's kids, she had lived here originally, he hadn't come here until after the war had started, and had stayed.

"You can trust Bernhard," he said.

"Oh ya?" Ingrid said.

"You could during the war, too, even though his parents are in jail."

"Oh ya?" Ingrid said.

"For treason."

He placed the breadboard on the table, covered with cheese and sliced meat, and butter and cups and cutlery. Ingrid said that was a lot of food. He burst into laughter and said he wasn't used to having guests, and he didn't have any milk, what would the toddler like? Ingrid said bread and water and placed Kaja on her lap and put the toy car on the table in front of her, cast around for something to talk about, but didn't find anything, and his silence was unbearable. She said it was good food, and the tea, too. He said she should add some sugar. She added some sugar to the tea and stirred it with a small spoon, and gave some to Kaja to try, another teaspoonful . . . And he asked if she was going to put Kaja to bed first.

"First? Hva does tha mean?" Ingrid said.

He laughed, revealing regular, white teeth, and said that he had been chopping wood in order to have something to do, at the wrong time of the year, he still mowed the grass, at the right time of the year, even though he didn't have any animals, he was planning to sell the farm, to Bernhard maybe.

Ingrid didn't understand what he was getting at, and felt the same confusion as in the war, when people were coming apart at the seams, or completely disintegrating, saliva had collected in her mouth.

"There's a cot upstairs," he said. "You can find your own way. Meanwhile I'll clear up."

Ingrid picked up Kaja, went over to the door, turned and asked why he had been expecting her.

"He told me about you."

"Hvur could he do that?"

"I can speak Russian."

"Hvar did tha learn that?"

"In Tsyp-Navalok."

Ingrid felt like asking where Tsyp-Navalok was, but instead she asked what Alexander had said about her.

"You know what," he said, and left it at that.

Well, that's something at least, Ingrid thought, and asked what his name was.

"Henrik," he said. "And you're Ingrid Barrøy."

She gave a start, mumbled an inaudible thank you and went up to the attic and stood stock-still in the middle of the floor in a large, airy room, until she began to cry, as she didn't have the strength to do anything else, since what she was seeking could not be found, no matter how far she walked.

There was a bowl of lukewarm water on the table by the window, as though *that*, too, had been expecting her, next to two neatly folded towels. Ingrid undressed Kaja, got her ready for bed, and sang to her. And when she had fallen asleep, Ingrid didn't dare to go down again, she couldn't even get up from the bed. Ingrid Marie Barrøy had arrived at her destination, and it was just as bad as she had not even dared to believe.

25

A new morning had left a film of dust over the window – the yellow mainland dust that settled on eyes and glass and skin and clothes – and someone had opened it. There was a children's paradise of pictures on the walls, of animals standing still. Shadows lay like down in the corners of the room. Ingrid became aware of the blankets lying over her, the width of the bed, a marital bed, which she hadn't noticed the evening before. Beside her, Kaja's breath rose from the green cradle that she herself had placed her in, and, outside, the swallows and insects played.

But Ingrid hadn't spread the blankets over herself, and she was dressed, her plait had come loose and her hair lay in tangled cascades across the broad pillow which smelled of soap and dried hay. She lay in a state of suspension – and she felt that Alexander was alive.

She heard the sound of an engine die. Then voices. She got up and tiptoed over to the window and looked down at two men talking in hushed tones, Bernhard sitting on a tractor and Henrik standing beside it, gesticulating with his black glove towards the racks that still bore hay in the field down to the valley. She could also hear the stream from here at the window.

They were laughing at something, of the two men Bernhard was the louder. He started up the tractor and drove out of the yard. Henrik went into the barn and returned with a pitchfork, then disappeared in the same direction.

Ingrid brushed and plaited her hair and went down to the kitchen, which looked as though it had just been cleaned. A milk jug in the middle of the table with beads of condensation and a brass handle. She found a coffee pot in the cupboard beside the cooker and stood staring at the six knobs and four electric hotplates, and made up her mind to wait, because she couldn't decide whether she could bring herself to show her face to Bernhard, even though he already knew she had spent the night there.

She leaned over the sink and washed with soap, dried herself on a tea towel and stood at the foot of the stairs listening for Kaja, but there wasn't a sound.

She went outside into the sunshine and down the field and watched the two men fork load after load of hay onto a set of iron teeth that stuck out from behind the P.T.O. shaft on the tractor and which she would later learn was called a buck rake. They looked like father and son, chatting and laughing and waving at her, and continued work as though she weren't there or as though she had always been there. Ingrid could feel a blush of shame spreading across her face as well as relief that no-one could see this.

She went back up to the house and sat on the bed waiting for Kaja to wake. She got to her feet and went into the room next door. It was like the one she had slept in, but the colours were different, the tone of the furniture too. She continued into the next room, which was like hers. And a different colour again. Neither of the rooms was in use, although the beds were not only made but covered with crocheted bedspreads. She saw another door, which connected the two houses and took her into another corridor with three more doors and a stairwell at the end. She opened the first door and found no sign of him. She sat down on the bed and wasn't sure if she could detect a scent, the one smell she missed more than any other, that of a winter's night in the North Chamber on Barrøy.

A blackout blind was rolled up above the window. She opened a cupboard and saw bed linen and towels laid out in military order. A small brass cross with one slanted bar above the door, a rose-painted bookcase and books in a script she couldn't read. Not a trace of anything *else*. She went out and closed the door, turned and went straight back in, thinking she could detect the same smell, and this time she was more certain, but once again it was gone.

She walked back to the other part of the house, down to the kitchen, boiled some coffee and put cups and saucers on a tray, scanned the cupboards in vain for anything resembling a cake or a *lefse*, decided she wasn't going to make waffles, and took the tray down to the field and placed it on the stubble as soon as the men saw her. She turned and walked quickly back, blushing now, too, and Kaja was awake.

26

Henrik Markus Axelsen met the escaped Russian P.O.W. Alexander Mihailovich Nizhnikov at Angle Station 2 one night between Christmas and New Year in 1944, he didn't remember the exact date, nor did anyone else.

Angle Station 2 is a point on the cableway between Kongsmoen and Namdalen at which it turns twelve degrees. The concrete foundations and footings of two private houses had been laid and between them a Sami family had erected a lavvu tent from birch poles and canvas tarpaulins which was to protect the building materials. It lay low on the ground, with a fireplace, covered by layer upon layer of carpets and reindeer pelts in which six adults and adolescents and three small wriggling children sat in the light of a flaming hearth. From the vent at the top rose smoke that no German occupation forces would be able to spot in bad weather.

When Alexander Nizhnikov staggered in at midnight on this forgotten date, blotchy-faced and distraught, sweaty and frozen stiff, unleashing a stream of incomprehensible words from between chattering teeth, the Sami thought they were being haunted by a spectre and were about to throw him out. But Henrik Axelsen woke up and explained to them that the man was Russian and needed food and warmth, he's one of us, he's escaped from the Germans.

When the storm abated, a good twenty-four hours later, the two men walked further down the Namdalen valley, in front of two sleds pulled by the family's eldest sons to erase their tracks. Unseen, they crossed the Namsen river, where it split into three branches, two of which were frozen over, and lay in bivouac for a day and a night. But lighting a fire was unwise so they had to let their clothes dry on their bodies. They walked along the cableway route through the mountains to Skorovas for another day and night, and were given shelter by the foreman of the local laundry, a prominent resistance man without a name. They spent the next twenty-four hours so close to the power station that generated electricity for the mines that on their further journey to Vollheim they joked that they had lost their hearing, because they kept saying *sto, sto, sto,* which means "what, what, what" in Russian, Henrik had no problem remembering this particular detail, they spoke in whispers, that was why they could not hear each other, he said, and they laughed at that.

For the first time they were walking in warm clothes. For the first time Henrik also started to reflect on the age gap between them, they could have been father and son, and the son was so brim-full of life that it rubbed off on a father who many a time in the last year had been on the point of giving up – *that's* not something you forget either, that it was Alexander who saved *me*, and not me *him*.

On this stretch of the journey the young man also declared for the first time – "If I've survived Titovka and Litza and Blood Road and the *Rigel*, I'll also manage to struggle my way through the Norwegian wilds. This is nothing."

They continued walking along the main cableway route, each in their own tractor rut, met no-one until they were received in Vollheim by Herman and Mariann and accommodated in the boathouse by the lake, where at night they could fire up a furnace.

But they didn't get any further.

And the days went by.

The lake isn't passable at times when the ice is forming in the autumn and it melts in the spring, and these periods can last for weeks on end. They didn't want to attempt walking through the metre-deep snow in the forests along the southern bank under any circumstances, so they lay low in the boathouse for more than a week.

There they also met two others. Henrik had heard talk of one of them, a certain Lauritz Myrland, and considered him reliable, as did Herman and Mariann.

But the second man wasn't known to any of them, and he behaved oddly, digging and delving for information about who they were, where they came from – details no-one gives in war-time – the routes they had taken, their network of contacts, and when they asked what his name was, he answered Håkon, as though he couldn't even be bothered to make up some cock-and-bull story, did Ingrid understand?

Ingrid said she did.

They also thought he laughed too much, and there wasn't much to laugh about here, Myrland had been forced to leave his wife and three children in Namsos at a moment's notice, while Henrik had been on the run for close on a year, after a failed operation on the island of Arnøya in northern Troms, not knowing anything about what had happened to his comrades, whether they had been killed, taken prisoner by the Germans or had managed to make it back to the Soviet Union. And Alexander? He had survived the bloodiest battles on the Northern Front, then seen almost two years in the camps in Korgen and Botn, surrounded by death, hunger and brutality. Then the *Rigel*, being saved from death on Barrøy and, not least, the march across the mountains from Kongsmoen.

Then at last Herman Vollheim said it was safe for them to continue on their way, on one of the first days in the New Year, the ice could carry them, at least as far as Stallvika, the temperatures had been sub-zero for a long time now, and there was no wind. Mariann was still hesitant about letting the fugitives go, after the disaster with her children she was hysterical about this ice, and Herman was no longer completely sure himself, or perhaps he was allowing himself to be influenced by his daughter.

171

So we decided to take a chance.

We tied a rope to one another and walked onto the ice ten or twelve metres apart. At first everything went well, but then the ice began to creak ominously, perhaps because it was packing, we shouted to each other and decided to head towards the southern bank and monitor the conditions.

We were now so far from Stallvika that we took a risk and lit a fire. It was a few degrees below zero and there was no wind. We discussed whether to walk the five or six kilometres back to Vollheim, we knew the ice would carry us that way, and wait in the boathouse for a few more days. Or whether we should battle our way the thirty kilometres or so eastwards through the forests – the lake was no longer an option, only a few hundred metres ahead we could see open water.

Unfortunately we chose the forest, although I am hard put to remember how we came to that decision. The only thing I do remember clearly is that this Håkon had been strangely quiet, now we were also given a surname that none of us had asked for, nothing was as it should be about this man.

We waded through the snow, for one night and one day, and took turns to lead. It began to snow again, and we were finding it more and more difficult to make any progress. It wasn't until the following night that we found the cabin Herman had marked on our map. By then Alexander and I had been more or less carrying Lauritz the last few kilometres. Håkon was crawling on his hands and knees and none of us had the strength to eat or light a fire, we slumped beneath the animal hides and fell asleep. And when we woke up the following day, we were unable to carry on, which turned out to have fateful consequences. When we did eventually cross the border – the following day – and got to Lake Kvarnberg, we didn't meet our contact.

But at least the ice on the lake could carry our weight.

We found a ramshackle boathouse and decided to wait. It had become colder and we were getting short of food, so the mood was tetchy when our contact finally found us. He called himself Peder, but later I heard his name was Nikolas. He said he had followed our tracks until he saw the fire – we'd had to break down part of the wall to have some fuel to keep it going.

However, he refused to take "Håkon", with no other explanation than that he stank, with which pronouncement we actually agreed. But then he realised that Alexander was Russian and after that he didn't want anything to do with any of us. When we were off our guard he managed to escape on his skis.

The wind picked up, his tracks were covered over by the snow and the next day all we could do was walk back to the cabin by Lake Tunnsjø. When we arrived there, we were on our last legs. We lit a fire and ate the little food we had remaining and decided to have a good night's sleep and afterwards try to head south on the Norwegian side, towards a small farming community called

Kveila. It was about the same distance away as Herman and Mariann's, however there was a road to the place, which admittedly hadn't been cleared, but it was easier to negotiate than the forest. In addition, it followed the border, so we could quickly cross over if we were seen.

But now this Håkon completely lost his head, he didn't want to go south, he wanted to go back to Vollheim, and *we* should too, he insisted. We said he could do as he liked, but on his own. However, he realised this would mean certain death, in his state. He pulled out a gun, a German model, and tried to threaten us to follow his orders, he was in charge now and we could choose either to obey or be shot.

There were some small farms and houses around, in two of which we had seen lights. He wanted us to go to the nearest one and force them to give us food. Herman had warned us in the strictest terms about making contact with civilians out there; it could compromise the whole network.

We tried to talk Håkon round, he snorted, threatened and laughed at us in turn, and we gradually realised there was only one thing we could do, and I was the one who did it. Afterwards, in his rucksack we found circumstantial evidence that suggested he was in league with the Rinnan gang: some ration vouchers, a bank book with a photograph of him in uniform and of course a completely different name . . .

We tied rocks to his body, dragged it onto the ice and let the snow cover it. The following night we made our way to Kveila and were helped by some good people who took us in a horse-drawn sled to Nordli, where we were received by Roald and Katinka Høgmo. We stayed with them for more than a week. You've met them, of course . . .

"It war Alexander th't killed 'im," Ingrid said softly in the gathering darkness in the room, it had begun to dawn on her that Henrik wasn't telling the whole truth, either.

He was taken aback and stood up, appearing to reconsider, but said:

"No, it was *me*."

"Hvur did tha do it?"

"With a rock I'd grabbed from the hearth in the cabin."

Ingrid said there wasn't a hearth, there was a stove, she'd been there.

He said there were rocks under the stove that were used for placing on the saucepans, and *on* the stove, to retain heat.

Ingrid said she had a feeling he was still here.

"Who?"

"Alexander."

"*Here* in this house?"

"Yes."

"Are you crazy? He left more than a year ago."

Why then did she have this sensation of nausea again, this stench around her, Ingrid asked, it wasn't only caused by memories but by lies.

"How should I know?" he said, his eyes not wavering a

millimetre from hers.

Ingrid quickly asked if Alexander had been married in Russia.

"It's called the Soviet Union."

"Ya, and?"

"No," he said in a softer voice. "But he had a sweetheart. Maria. She was studying to be an architect . . ."

"*Had?*" Ingrid said.

"Erm . . ." he said, puzzled.

"A don't believe tha!"

He asked her why.

Ingrid had to stand up to make sure the ice was holding. Her feet were cold and stiff. She turned her back on him and walked barefoot into the star-filled darkness, which had no business being there at this time of year, inhaled so deeply that her lungs quivered, then walked slowly around the barn, saw constellations she had never seen before, stopped, dried her tears and hurried slowly back inside, and by then he had left the kitchen.

Upstairs, she heard footsteps from the other part of the house. A distant door slammed. She wondered whether she should go to the switch and turn off the light before she went to bed or whether to leave it on. She saw Alexander's smile as he rowed away from Barrøy, that white wedge in the night, and felt a shiver run through her arms and legs as she reflected that Henrik didn't belong here any more than she did, he was a foreigner on his own property. Then she switched off the light and groped her way up the stairs and into the room where Kaja was sleeping, wan moonlight lying like a white tablecloth over the floorboards.

27

It never rained in these parts. Henrik Axelsen and Ingrid Barrøy were standing on a sloping field in dazzling sunshine coiling hay-rack wire and easing poles out of the ground before laying them on the buck rake Bernhard had left there. Beside them, Kaja was crawling around on a blanket, which was too small. Henrik supported himself on a pole and said, gazing into the mountains, that he and Alexander had parted company with Lauritz at Høgmo farm in Nordli, and then they had *not* gone towards the nearest border crossing, but back through the Norwegian mountains, heading for Snåsa.

Ingrid knew what that meant and asked why they hadn't told the people at Høgmo where they were going.

"We didn't trust anyone. And if this Peder – or Nikolas – knew what he was talking about at Lake Kvarnberg, the border would've been closed anyway."

"Rielly?" Ingrid said.

He glowered at her and asked if she was questioning his version of events *again*.

Ingrid hastened to say no.

"But it was too far. And I was too old. We broke into three different cabins and slept outside in the snow for four nights. That was when I damaged my hand, first with an axe, the frost did the rest."

He held up his hand, loosened the straps and showed her a crippled little finger and a bright red band around his wrist, like a second glove, of blood. He said he wore the glove not because of the pain but because he didn't want to see his wounds, they reminded him of winter, he couldn't tolerate winters any longer, then strapped the glove back on and said:

"You're strange."

"No, A'm not," Ingrid said, and asked again if he was sure it was him who had killed Håkon.

"You don't give up, do you."

Ingrid stared. "Yes," he said. "The others held him and I struck him."

"An' th' gun?"

"He didn't even have time to release the safety catch."

Ingrid averted her eyes. Henrik told her to look at him.

"Hvafor?"

"So that I can see you understand what I'm saying."

"Does tha teik me f'r a clot?"

"Far from it. I think you're from another planet."

"Hva does tha mean?"

Henrik Axelsen suddenly seemed like everyone else. And since he hadn't answered her question, Ingrid asked it again.

Henrik said she came from an island; she didn't need to talk to anyone.

"An' tha's fra Finnmark," Ingrid said.

He laughed and said:

"Good point."

Ingrid said she didn't know what to say when she spoke to him; she just said whatever came into her head.

"You really *are* strange," he said, sat down, and gave the impression it would be a while before he was able to continue.

Ingrid said that now she was standing while he was sitting.

She also said she was looking straight at him.

He gave a resigned smile, told her to sit as well, and she didn't need to look at him like that. She sat down.

"The hardest night we spent outdoors was down in Snåsa, where we'd chosen a house that seemed to be empty. But we had to be sure, and in the end when Alexander eventually smashed the cellar window, he did it for my sake. It took me several days to recover. We ate whatever food we could find there ... jam, flat bread, tins ... we slept on mattresses on the floor, didn't light a fire, moved around in complete darkness and scarcely looked outside, all the while feeling that the longer we stayed there, the greater the risk we'd be caught. But there was a telephone in the house, so I got hold of my sister in Oslo, whom I'd rung from Høgmo as well, she was the one who suggested I come to this farm, which was empty. She also thought that Bernhard was reliable, even if his parents weren't, Belteren has always been at war."

Ingrid asked him what his sister's name was.

"What's that got to do with anything?"

Ingrid said nothing. He said: "After three days in the house we'd worked out the times of the trains and one night sneaked on board a goods train to Trondheim. There, we bought some clothes with the Norwegian money I'd brought with me from the Soviet Union, and slept one night at a hotel, posing as everyday commercial travellers, it was unbelievable, white sheets, hot water, food . . . we were able to see to our hands, we were new-born, we almost killed ourselves laughing, we had our lives back. The following day we bought tickets, caught the train and made our way here without a hitch."

Ingrid didn't ask any of the questions she had on the tip of her tongue.

He appeared to notice, leaned back on his elbows and said everything was fine for the first few months, but when the ground began to thaw, Alexander became restless. We didn't have a radio, but we heard from Bernhard that soon it would all be over . . .

"He wanted t' go heim?"

"Yes, he wanted to go home. I imagine it wears you down walking in endless circles up there in the loft. And Bernhard's father kept coming up and sniffing around. Sooner or later the idiot would twig."

"So tha wanted 'im t' go?"

Henrik paused to reflect.

"I suppose I did."

Ingrid laid a hand on his glove and said that Alexander couldn't stay on Barrøy, either.

He looked straight at her and said calmly:

"We'll never know, neither you, nor I. That's what torments us."

Ingrid nodded and knew what had made it possible for her to let Alexander leave the island: the conviction that it would be possible to find him again, one day, but now she realised it wasn't conviction, it wasn't even a hope, it was fear, and cowardice too.

She got to her feet and walked onto the grassy slope and listened to the stream behind the bushes, beneath the low, blue mountains resembling breakers in a calm, milky sea. She had asked Henrik what Alexander had said about her, and he had answered "you know" in a way that made it impossible for her to ask again.

She turned and opened her mouth to speak, but he had sat Kaja on his lap and leaned her against his thighs, they were playing and babbling. Ingrid heard her laughing and saw him search for a tooth in her mouth, saw him say something, he was studying Kaja closely and knew who she was, it was unbearable.

Ingrid went down to the stream and spotted a log cabin between the trees, a mill and a grey, wooden channel, with a sluice gate at the end that led from the stream to a waterwheel that was motionless. She lifted the sluice gate, drops trickled through the cracks in the wood, but the buckets on the wheel filled and it began to move slowly, creaking on its own axis.

She heard a bird of prey through the sound of the rushing water. A ewe and two lambs came down to the bank, followed by two more sheep, none of them with a bell. She watched them steadily graze their way down a path they themselves must have made. By now Henrik was standing at her side with Kaja in his arms and he told her that after the war a camp had been set up in the south of the country, Alexander had probably gone there, a German concentration camp that was now being used to house these so-called displaced persons, P.O.W.s, soldiers, deserters, refugees, Russians, Yugoslavs, Poles, collaborators, the debris of war.

Ingrid looked at him.

"*Probably?*"

"Yes, he left without a word, in May last year, but he knew about the camp. Bernhard had told me about it and since then I haven't heard a thing."

"An' hva does that mean?" Ingrid said.

"I don't know. Thousands of these wretches have been sent back – repatriation, they call it – tens of thousands . . . He's probably in Leningrad now."

Ingrid slowly shook her head.

He asked her what was going through her head *now*.

She grabbed Kaja, pulled off her socks and let her stand in the channel by the mill wheel.

He said that the water came from the mountains and was cold. Kaja might get ill.

Ingrid stuck her finger in the water and said that she liked being dipped into the sea, which is much colder. He smiled, turned and set off up on the path to the field. She called after him, why was everyone so frightened of remembering?

He stopped.

"Maybe we're more frightened of what *others* might remember."

Ingrid thought this sounded like something Dr Hübner would say.

"A remember ev'rythin'," she shouted.

"You may think you do," he said and carried on up the slope.

Ingrid sat Kaja on a tussock and held her feet until they were dry, met her gaze and thought she received a signal, pulled on her socks, raised her onto her shoulders and followed the sheep track up alongside the stream until she was above the treeline and continued towards the bare mountains. She walked barefoot in the heather and silvery moss, rested and went on, there was no path and no wind, the babbling stream was gone, the air was as dry as dust, and this was beginning to feel like a hike again, she was on the verge of smiling and had no idea why.

But nothing happened when she reached a flat area of high ground with a cairn that looked as if it had been built by children playing. She could see further in all directions than she had ever seen across a sea. The silence became even more profound. She looked Kaja in the eye, and Kaja looked at her, and she thought, I'll turn around now and go back down. To a man who hadn't become any easier to understand during these days, there was also something enthralling about all this, it was one of the forces that kept her here on this mysterious mainland.

Evening was drawing in as Ingrid came back down to the farmyard, where Henrik was standing with one foot on the hay-rack poles bundled together on the buck rake and talking to two apparent strangers, who turned out to be Bernhard and a young girl with long, fair hair that billowed over round, plump shoulders, both she and Bernhard were dressed in their finest clothes, as though they were going to a party, they were laughing about something or other.

Bernhard nodded amiably to her. Henrik told the fair-haired girl that Ingrid was Ingrid and Ingrid heard the name Siri and shook her hand and introduced Kaja, who was still sitting on her shoulders, and at once saw Siri's smile wander. Ingrid had instinctively moved to Henrik's side, so that they faced each other as two couples, an older and a younger couple talking about something confidential.

Ingrid blushed and excused herself by saying that Kaja was hungry, spun round, went into the kitchen, turned on the tap above the sink, waited until the water was cold and splashed her face with it.

Over the supper table the same evening she said that Henrik could sleep with her that night. He looked at her strangely and said:

"That's nice. I'll think about it."

They didn't say anything else to each other during the meal, just spoke a few words to Kaja, who was sitting between two hard cushions on a plank of wood Henrik had laid over the arms of a chair and was patiently chewing the bits of bread they gave her. Then he did say something after all, he said it wasn't only her eyes, her gestures and her smile were Alexander to a T, it was like seeing him alive, a dead man.

Ingrid jumped up and shouted, no, he isn't, no, he's not, snatched Kaja and ran up to her room, and stood there as if paralysed until Kaja roused her with a scream.

He didn't come to her in the night. Ingrid was cold, fetched another blanket and was still cold, lifted Kaja from her cradle, curled up around her and wondered why they had stayed in their separate beds all these nights.

28

The rain came down in sheets and turned the farmyard into brown mud. Ingrid heard the sea and saw the darkness and jumped up to close the window. She looked down on a yard in tumult, lightning snarling above bowed, quaking trees, heard thunder and the next moment saw Henrik running naked from the porch to the barn. He lost his footing and fell headlong, rolled over onto his back in the mud and grass and broke into an eerie laughter.

He got up and stood bent over, cursed out loud, suddenly stiffened and looked up, saw Ingrid and waved despairingly with his ungloved hand.

Ingrid tore open the door, ran down and threw herself around his neck and said she didn't love him. He buried his face in her neck and said he didn't love her, either. They stood holding each other, staggered and fell, Ingrid in Mariann's dress, which she had washed the day before. She knew he might end up hitting her, instead of which he lay limp, like a sack, and groaned that he couldn't bear her, she should let go of him.

Ingrid said no, and held on to him.

He lay with his face half in the mud, a man who has survived a war, wailing. Ingrid held him until his shaking subsided, not knowing whether to kiss him or drink the rainwater in her ear.

"That's enough," he gasped.

"No," Ingrid said.

"That's enough," he repeated, and rested his head on her arm. Ingrid asked him if he was cold, and didn't let go. He said, no, and didn't move. They lay there until she heard a child howling, until the sounds were audible in *his* body, too. Then they got up and mumbled apologies and went through separate doors into the double house as the rain lashed down in the void after them.

For the rest of the day they busied themselves indoors and when they met they said, it'll soon stop raining, good job we've got the hay in . . . Ingrid made some coffee, which they drank in their separate rooms, played with Kaja, sang and washed and tidied up a kitchen that was becoming smaller and smaller. Henrik came and dropped a pair of shoes on the floor in front of her and said they had belonged to his sister, Ingrid couldn't trudge around in miners' boots, that wasn't very lady-like. Ingrid asked what "lady-like" meant, but he didn't answer. She tried them on, they fitted. And again that evening she said across the supper table that he could come to her in the night.

But he didn't.

Ingrid got up at midnight and went into the other part of the house and knocked on the fourth door.

"Come in."

He was sitting in the wing chair by the window. On a little table stood a full bottle of spirits and an empty glass. He told her to sit down. There was only the bed to sit on. Ingrid asked why he hadn't come to her. He said:

"I don't know."

Ingrid stayed on her feet and asked what his sister's name was.

"Elisabeth."

She asked why he hadn't found out what had happened to his comrades after the failed operation on Arnøya.

He looked surprised, but didn't answer.

She asked what he wasn't telling her.

He squirmed.

She asked what *he* was frightened of discovering, because that was why he was still hiding here, wasn't it?

He told her to shut up.

Ingrid scanned the shelves of books piled flat where they should have been upright, a desk that looked as if it belonged to a district magistrate. Oh, yes, there was something else she wanted to ask – whether Mariann and Herman knew they had killed this man, Håkon, at the eastern end of Lake Tunnsjø.

He asked why she was interested, then answered angrily:

"I assume so. We told Roald Høgmo anyway and urged

him to find out whether Håkon was an infiltrator."

Ingrid stared into space. He said: "And presumably he was, although I never heard."

"Tha didn't answer th' letters, did tha?"

"I don't get letters, I've told you. And why don't you ask about the *Rigel*? They were fried alive on board that ship, thousands of innocent men. Afterwards the Germans shot several of the survivors because they couldn't bear to hear their screams. No-one wants to remember that."

Ingrid didn't understand.

"They were only *Russians*," he said impatiently. 'The world's taken a wrong turn now, everything's being rewritten, things are forgotten and falsified, this peace is just lies, how the hell can you pretend it's not?"

Ingrid said she wasn't interested in politics.

He said he had realised that, got up and went over to a rose-painted cabinet, took a glass and passed it to her, poured and said that Alexander and four others had managed to clamber on board a lifeboat, along with a German officer. They had drifted aimlessly through the storm until they hit an islet and the boat was smashed, his four comrades had died, from the frost or their injuries . . . But a dirty-white raft made of planks and oil drums drifted ashore and on it they were able to reach . . .'

"Barrøy."

"If you say so. He couldn't pronounce the name and by then there wasn't much life left in the German . . .'

"Tha remembered th' name when A came hier," Ingrid said. "Barrøy."

"Well, maybe. 'Ingrid' rang a bell anyway. Maybe 'Barrøy' too. I don't remember."

Right, Ingrid said brusquely, and now she could go home, thanks to him, this man who had been so honest with her.

He was taken aback:

"Home?"

"Tha said he war deed?"

He shook his head in exasperation, stood up, went to the desk and pulled out a drawer, took a pile of letters and dropped them in her lap. All Ingrid could decipher was Leningrad, some numbers and the Soviet Union.

"I wrote them," he said. "And they came back, all of them."

Ingrid drank the spirit neat and asked, why do you think that is?

He took a deep breath and said in an irritated tone:

"Don't you understand anything?"

"No."

"*Perhaps he didn't want to have any more to do with us!*"

"Hvafor?"

"He has his Maria, you have to get that into your head. He just wants to forget about us."

"Hvafor, hvafor, hvafor?" Ingrid persisted, and in a changed voice Henrik said he was the only person Alexander had been able to talk to.

Ingrid sent him a quizzical look.

He said he was the only person who knew the full truth about Alexander's hands – they were burned because he, together with fifteen hundred other prisoners, had been in the hold of the *Rigel* when it was bombed and set ablaze, and he had managed to stay alive inside a glowing, red-hot, iron tube, none of the others had, this man wanted to live.

Ingrid grabbed the bottle, filled her glass, emptied it in one draught and slumped down on the bed. Henrik knelt down beside her and removed the hands she discovered she had covered her face with.

"That's the way it is," he said calmly, holding her in his cold, coarse hands, the glove was hard and rough, the scars around his elbow stood out in the darkness. Ingrid pulled herself free, ran into the corridor and back to her room, noticed Herman Vollheim's watch showing five minutes past one and didn't know where she was.

But Kaja was asleep in a cradle she recognised, she saw that the window was open and that it had stopped raining. She recognised the walls and pictures of animals and lay down shaking, and then saw Barrøy and Alexander when she found him in the barn, the images that never changed, stared at them and studied them, now Vollheim's watch showed half past two and there was a knock at the door.

Ingrid said, "Come in."

Henrik came in with the bottle, which was half empty, sat

in the chair by the window and said nothing. Ingrid could feel that her eyes were dry and asked in a voice that carried through the darkness whether he wanted to lie down beside her. He said he would sit. Ingrid made out his silhouette against the window and heard Kaja breathing. He got up, came over and lay down behind her, his arms wrapped around her, fully clothed. She took his hands in hers and held them against her stomach and heard him repeat into the nape of her neck that she was strange. She held his glove with both hands and didn't fall asleep until he had got up in the first rays of sunlight and tiptoed out of the room on silent feet.

29

I ngrid had found a sack of flour in the pantry and was going to do some baking. Henrik came up behind her and said cheerfully *he* usually did that, he had been a baker in a former life. Ingrid could feel his breath on the hairs on the back of her neck and asked him how many lives he'd had. He didn't answer.

He played with Kaja while Ingrid baked.

He talked about the wife he had lost to T.B. fifteen years before, about Finnmark and his grandfather's freighter that plied the Archangel route, about his training in Oslo and a stay in England, which hadn't led to anything, a period in Stockholm, which hadn't lived up to expectations either. He said – as if this had anything to do with the matter – that he had never been a farmer, but now that was what he was in the process of becoming nonetheless.

Ingrid didn't appear to understand what he was driving at and asked what a partisan was.

"Resistance folk in Finnmark who worked for the Russians, for the N.K.V.D. But I was too old. It's terrible to be old . . ."

Ingrid said that now he sounded like an old biddy. He asked if she had begun to hate him for his evasiveness. Ingrid said, no, and put the loaves into the oven and asked once again why he was still in hiding. He said:

"Do you never get tired of asking questions?"

She shrugged and asked how well he knew Mariann and Herman Vollheim, and got to hear a repeat of what he had already said, listened to him talking about his sons, whom he hadn't seen for years, they weren't like him, neither in their politics, nor in any other way. But he didn't give any examples of these differences, and Ingrid didn't ask, she told him to tell her about the last day before Alexander disappeared.

"From here?"

"Ya, hva did thas talk about?"

But they were interrupted by a shout from Kaja on the floor. He laughed and lifted her onto the table and held her under her armpits so that she could stand. And Ingrid sensed he needed the time it took to lift the child. She heard him mumble that she shouldn't worry about Alexander. He was at home with his Maria now; they just had to accept it.

Ingrid said she didn't believe any of this.

He sat Kaja down and marched off like an angry soldier from a battle he couldn't be bothered to win. And Ingrid was left wondering if it was right that *he* was the one who had gone and she was the one to stay.

*

That night, too, he lay behind her, his arms wrapped around her. Now they were naked, and when they got up, they dressed in the light, with their backs to each other.

There was a wash-house in the cellar, where wool was spun and there was a large boiler, in which clothes were washed, as well as three enormous tubs beneath a broad window it was impossible to see through, it had been sand-blasted. Ingrid washed herself and Kaja in the biggest of them and washed their clothes in the middle one. She also washed Henrik's clothes, his shirts and trousers and underwear, so they hung beside nappies and tops and Mariann Vollheim's dress on a line running between the raised storehouse and the barn, a family of three, there for all to see.

He came and knocked and said through the closed door that there was a sauna on the farm, he didn't know how it worked, but would find out in the course of the day. Ingrid interpreted this as an invitation and said, yes.

That same evening they each sat swathed in a towel on a wooden bench in a small hut opposite the mill watching Kaja playing naked on the wet stone floor between two zinc buckets that she could splash about in. Henrik suggested Ingrid stay at the farm and teach him how to be a farmer. Ingrid repeated that she had to go home, she was calmer now, even the smell from the mysterious room had gone, the smell of a winter's night on Barrøy. Then it occurred to her that Alexander's hands had been so badly damaged that he would never have been able to touch her in the way a man should, and this seemed important.

"You've lived through a whole war," Henrik said, interrupting her thoughts. "Without understanding a single thing."

Ingrid turned in the grey light and saw a handsome man with high cheekbones and distinctive features, a lean, muscular man with a tiny, pulsating heart under the skin of his left cheek, which also throbbed when he slept.

She leaned forward, kissed it and asked what *he* had understood.

He shouted that the war had ruined everything, got up and threw the contents of one bucket over the stove, making it hiss, and left.

Ingrid sat back, motionless, and watched Kaja banging the ladle on the floor. Henrik returned with a full bucket, smiled as though nothing had happened, discovered he was naked as he stood there in the steam, wrapped a towel around himself and crept like a cat onto the bench beside her. Ingrid noticed that she was crying and that she had been doing so for a while. He said he couldn't go back to Finnmark, he was stuck in this Nazi-loving hole, during the war it had been the safest place in the country, now it was absolute hell, was there no way Ingrid could stay?

She replied quietly that it had become too hot for Kaja, got up and walked naked into the summer night with Kaja in her arms, and she felt goosebumps forming as he called after her that Alexander had not only saved *him*, but also *her*.

"But to what end?!"

She went up to her room and dressed herself and Kaja, pottered around doing nothing of any importance, and went down to the kitchen and prepared dinner. He didn't join her.

They ate slowly.

Ingrid cleared up, put Kaja to bed and went out again in the artificial summer darkness and heard shouting from the barn, the stamping of boots, the rattle of chains and glass being smashed. She went back in and up to her room and lay waiting. She heard a door bang in the other part of the house, but no footsteps. She told herself that she mustn't fall asleep, and had to sit upright in order to stay awake. She fell asleep and dreamt about rocks blocking her way and unrecognisable faces, when she suddenly realised what she ought to have realised as soon as she walked through the gate of the farm.

She got up and ran over into the other house, tore open the door and threw herself on him in bed and shouted that he had to tell her the truth.

He awoke with a splutter and tried to push her away. Ingrid held on tight and hissed that he had to tell her about Alexander and Mariann.

"What do you mean?"

"'Tha asked if she'd children but tha knew the'd drowned in th' leik!"

There was a long silence.

"Oh, my God," he gasped.

Ingrid screamed that Alexander hadn't slept in the boathouse with the other fugitives, but with Mariann.

At first he said, no, twice, swept her aside with surprising ease, sat up and drew his hands across his face as if to tear away a mask. Ingrid sat cross-legged on the floor and heard him mumble – well, well, so now she knew. But don't worry about it, it doesn't mean anything.

Ingrid didn't answer. He said sorry and explained that Mariann was the way she was and usually got what she wanted.

"An' '*im*?" Ingrid shouted. "Did he get what he war after an' all?"

"It doesn't mean anything, I said. Just a young lad who wants to live a bit."

"He war twenty-two."

"And you're thirty-five, thirty-six ...?"

"War he in 'er bed ev'ry night?"

"I don't remember ... no, not the first night."

"An' Herman knew?"

"Yes ... I assume so."

Ingrid heard the sound of bare feet on lacquered floorboards and glimpsed a shadow in front of the rose-painted cabinet with the glasses and spirits. She heard him open it, remove a bottle and take a long drink. His feet reappeared in her field of vision and she heard him ask her if she wanted some. She said, no, and that he had become only half a man.

He gave a hollow laugh, turned and slumped back onto the bed.

Ingrid glanced up at the tiny clock ticking under the skin of his cheek.

"Come and lie down," he said wearily.

Ingrid didn't stir.

"He did what he *had* to do. He's a survivor, Ingrid, now he's also a Hero of the Soviet Union. The Russians take care of their own."

Ingrid said calmly:

"It warn't that bit about th' children."

"What wasn't that bit about the children . . . ?"

She mumbled that it hadn't been his slip of the tongue in the kitchen that had opened her eyes to what had gone on between Mariann and Alexander. She had suspected it the morning Mariann blocked her way at Høgmo farm, the way Mariann said that he *must* have survived the hike across the mountains, her face, the freckles and the twitching scar at the corner of the mouth of a beautiful woman who had lost everything, who had been given her life back by a Russian fugitive, whom she had also lost.

Henrik gazed at her, waiting.

Ingrid got to her feet and stood still, her heart racing. She went out, closed the door carefully behind her and made her way back to the other house with a sense that she must not sleep now either, a hazy, alien feeling.

She switched on the light and lay looking up at a five-armed chandelier with small flower-shaped shades. One was crooked and had a brown stain. She climbed on the bed and unscrewed the light bulb, then placed it on the bedside table and gazed at the quivering silver filaments behind the pear-shaped glass. The chandelier was now lop-sided. She got up and switched off the light, stood by the window and stared out until the gleaming fields of Belteren farm came into focus. Then she returned to the bed, closed her eyes and waited for him to come. But he didn't.

30

Ingrid got up early and stole over to the other house, heard the sound of restless breathing behind a closed door and went back and sat down to write a farewell letter, thanking him for whatever came to mind in the rush, and to her surprise it was much more than she had anticipated, she sat putting it off, and when it could be put off no longer, she left the letter on the table by the window, rose to her feet and returned to his closed door in the other house, heard once more his restless breathing and stood there while nothing happened.

She went to fetch Kaja, who was still asleep, and the rucksack she had packed, and left the house on a day that bore every sign of being as dry and radiant as all the other days in this unchanging region, apart from the one day when it rained, when something happened that was beyond all her understanding.

She walked down the dusty road without feeling any eyes on her back and was passing Belteren farm when she heard a sound in the sky. She stopped and looked for a plane as the swallows chirruped above the yellow meadows that had become even lusher.

She heard another sound, of iron and tramping hooves, and was caught up by Bernhard on a horse-drawn carriage. He stopped and asked if she wanted a lift.

Ingrid said she was going to catch the bus down at the crossroads.

He smiled and said there were no buses today, it was Sunday.

Ingrid reluctantly stepped up and took a seat beside him and at that moment Kaja awoke. Bernhard smiled at her and said she was a pretty child and explained that he was going to pick up his mother from the railway station, she was ill and on compassionate leave, though he didn't mention anything about what she had been given leave from, he asked Ingrid if she was going to catch the train.

"Yes."

"South?"

"North."

He said she would have to wait a long time then.

Ingrid said if there was one thing she was good at it was waiting, so she would have to wait, she hadn't even left the place, as though Brynet farm too would be with her from now until eternity. Bernhard asked if she had enjoyed her time there and if she was related to Henrik.

Ingrid answered yes to both questions and said with her eyes fixed on the horse's back that she had travelled far and wide this summer, but still hadn't met anyone who was genuinely happy that the war was over.

He glanced sideways at her in surprise and said that *he* definitely was, now everything was going to settle down and return to how it had been.

"Tha understands ev'rythin' A say," Ingrid said.

"Yes," he said.

She thought he was like Daniel from Malvika, a man without any dark sides, and asked if he knew that Henrik had hidden someone at Brynet during the last winter of the war.

"I can't answer that," he said in a tone that made it impossible to determine whether he *couldn't* or he *wouldn't*.

Ingrid said the war didn't seem to be over after all then.

Again he glanced at her in surprise.

She stared at the dun horse's back, streaked with white sweat beneath the harness and reins, and said he would have to keep an eye on Henrik, he couldn't be on his own anymore.

"Oh?" Bernhard said. 'I've got more than enough to see to with my mother now."

Ingrid said:

"He's not meid t' bi a farmer."

"Isn't he . . . ?" Bernhard said.

Ingrid asked why he was still at Brynet, who was he hiding from?

Bernhard thought long and hard while Ingrid counted trees and milk ramps.

"He was receiving post by special courier right up until last summer," he said at length.

"Oh, yes?" Ingrid said.

Bernhard said hesitantly that the two comrades Henrik had been with on Arnøya had managed to make it back to the Soviet Union. They had walked through Sweden and Finland.

"Oh, yes?" Ingrid said.

"But they weren't welcomed as heroes. They were sent to camps, on Stalin's orders, and one was later shot as he attempted to escape."

"Oh, my God," Ingrid said, not daring to ask for further details about these orders. But she did ask whether they were Norwegians or Russians.

"Norwegians."

She managed to stifle a thank God. And Bernhard steered the horse around another bend and into shadow. It was a splendid carriage, painted glossy black with green wheel spokes and rims and golden embellishments on the sides. They heard the sound of running water. A flock of crows took to the air from a field to the left of the road. They passed more and more people walking in the same direction, Bernhard greeted them all, but not everyone greeted *him*, and they covered the last kilometres without saying a word to each other.

31

Ingrid Marie Barrøy entered yet another station building and saw three young men and one elderly man standing in a sort of queue at the ticket window. On the wall between the window and the door leading to the platform hung a glass-framed map of Norway. She stood in front of it and her eyes began to search for place names, roads, railway lines . . . a grey mark on the glass, left by thousands of fingertips over the point where she was, in the middle of the country and the summer. Through the window to the right she could see the southbound train arriving, it was 9:51, and passengers began to get on and off in the same orderly way as so many before them, at Formofoss, in Trondheim, at Røros . . .

Ingrid found Mysen at the bottom of the map and worked out that it was only possible to travel there via the capital, if you were going by train. At that moment she caught sight of Bernhard, who was helping an old woman in black and wearing a veil, down the steps of the middle coach, along with a crowd of onlookers who surrounded them and said things or shouted. Bernhard seemed ill at ease.

Ingrid cast a glance at the ticket window, there was only one young man left in the queue, there seemed to be some disagreement between those on either side of the glass partition. She walked into the sunlight, nodded to Bernhard as she passed. He didn't notice her. She stepped up into the same coach his mother had just left and sat down in an empty compartment, from which, through the window, she could see Bernhard and the old lady making their way through a crowd of people still yelling at them. He helped his mother up into the carriage, shouted something back and geed the horse out of the station yard as the train got up steam again. Once more Ingrid was heading in the wrong direction.

She sat staring out of the window at the new landscape until Kaja woke up, then took out her doll and sat her daughter in the middle of the seat opposite, held her there with her feet, tickling her with her toes, and asked if she was hungry.

Kaja smiled and shook the doll.

They looked at each other.

Ingrid opened her rucksack and took out the sketch pad: Mysen and the concentration camp and displaced persons and Russians and Poles . . . "the debris of war". As well as the name, Elisabeth, because that was the sister she believed Henrik had lied about, the owner of the shoes that were tidily placed on the floor below her knees and were the finest examples of footwear Ingrid had ever possessed.

*

Under the sketch pad there was a sheet of paper, wrapped around a cardboard box. Ingrid unfolded it and read that if she was on her way home now she would be the first person to have succeeded in putting the war behind her, congratulations.

If not, she should return to Brynet without delay, the farm needed her. In addition, Henrik regretted that he had said he didn't love her.

Ingrid noticed that he had elegant handwriting, with lots of formal loops and tails, which wasn't a feature of a farmer's style, and it irked her that she must have fallen asleep after all.

She opened the cardboard box and a small metal cylinder fell into her lap, it was a kind of cartridge with a screw cap. She undid it and another cylinder fell out, black with yellow capital letters and numbers and broad notched heads at the top and bottom. She shook it and tried to open it, gave up and put it back in the rucksack and re-read Henrik's letter, feeling almost the same as the first time, the rhythm of the train was beginning to have an effect on her – as an endless line of towering trees flashed by in the dusty light.

She counted the money she had left and had no idea how far it would take them, not to mention whether it would be enough to get them home. She wanted to leave the train again, but stayed where she was. She was about to feed Kaja when a young, fair-haired conductor without a cap came and tapped a ticket punch on the door, opened it with a tug and was plainly annoyed that she hadn't bought a ticket.

"You have to get one at the station," he shouted through the noise he had let into the compartment.

Ingrid shouted back that she hadn't had time.

"Then I'll have to write one," he shouted reproachfully.

Ingrid looked at him.

"Tha *can* write, can't tha?"

"There's nothing wrong with *my* head," he said, as if in a well-practised ritual, came into the compartment and closed the door, it was quieter now, and Ingrid told him where she was going, but on no account must it be via the capital.

He asked why not, that was where the train was going.

Ingrid looked at him.

He shook his head, glanced at Kaja and said, wait, disappeared and returned with a map, identical to the one she had seen on the station wall. With him he also had a pad and a pencil and a *Rutebok for Norge*, which included maps and all the bus and train times for the country. He sat down beside Kaja and said Ingrid should write out the ticket and find a route herself, by bus or whatever she preferred, for example, from Elverum, but he would strongly advise against her doing that.

Ingrid flicked through the pages and found a route she thought might be suitable, which consisted of four buses with relatively short waits and a circuitous stretch on foot. The conductor placed a broad fingernail in the column on the pad where she had to write, and she wrote.

But he didn't leave, and asked why they were going to Mysen.

Ingrid said she didn't know, which was true, she was searching for someone who might not be alive.

He gave a nervous laugh.

Ingrid fed Kaja. He watched with interest until the train pulled into another station, said Ingrid could keep the *Rutebok* and the map, and left. When Kaja fell asleep, Ingrid too was able to close her eyes. Mariann hadn't wanted Alexander to go across the ice, but she'd had no choice, because *he* wanted to.

32

Ingrid Marie Barrøy arrived at the former concentration camp, Sonderlager Mysen in light drizzle one night at the beginning of August 1946, after a tortuous journey by train and four buses, a long trek through two forests with white-washed farmhouses and ochre barns and gravel roads and paths, and at length with the help of a grumpy lorry driver who took her right to the door.

The camp lay shrouded in darkness, however, and no-one opened up, it didn't even look like a camp, it was night, it was overcast and something had happened over the last few days: her footsteps had become pointless, she had started worrying about the mowing season on the Barrøy islets, about the price of the rest of the down at the moment of truth, about the house that had to be painted by someone other than herself . . .

She pictured the whaler in the bay and Barbro's wry smile, Suzanne's resigned, restless face, Suzanne who was less suited to the island than anyone else, trapped as she was by both war and peace.

Ingrid had bargained for ten minutes with a farmer who

211

tried to sell her milk at an outrageous price and had walked on and eyed him from top to toe as the idiot he was. She had thought about the light nights in the north which now, slowly but surely, were turning into gloomy wildernesses, like the nights here in the south. She had seen semi-naked boys fishing in a reed-filled tarn where she was washing nappies. She had seen cows so brown and massive in the heat that they didn't have the energy to stand upright.

She had slept and walked with as many kilos on her back as on her stomach and had asked so many people the way that she couldn't distinguish one from the other. She had tramped further than anyone, through a country where no-one knew her and no-one would remember her and where the sound of a car approaching from behind and passing by, only to disappear in the dust ahead of them, had made her shed tears. She was standing on the edge of a precipice, but carried on. She didn't have enough energy for her own child's needs, she passed two milestones and saw a mother smacking her son. She walked through heavy, hazy heat, scanned endless cornfields and saw a gang of carpenters erecting a barn on the ruins of an old one. She heard the voice of a car mechanic, but didn't understand what he said because he couldn't be bothered to look up from the engine. And even though she realised again and again that she wasn't thinking about Alexander, she ploughed on in the shoes of an Elisabeth she would never know because it was still easier – though only just – to go forwards than backwards, she was no longer seeking the truth, her journey had become a desperate hunt for a turning point.

In the hours it took for the light to return, she sat erect on a bench in a bus shelter and slept restlessly with Kaja on her lap. At five o'clock in the morning a lorry juddered to a halt and a bundle of newspapers landed with a thump on the ground in front of her. The rain resembled swirling flour. Ingrid stared at the pile of paper and fresh newsprint. A young lad on a bike skidded to a stop in front of her, slit the twine with a penknife, filled his bags with newspapers and disappeared again without seeing her.

The drizzle eased off. The sun struggled through the clouds. Ingrid loved Kaja more than ever before, stood up, cold and stiff, and walked back to Sonderlager Mysen and banged on the gate, again without any response. She pressed a brass bell on the right-hand gatepost and there wasn't a sound. A gigantic floodlight came on, only to be extinguished again, as though it had worked out itself that it was daytime, and a man's hoarse voice asked through a hatch in the gate what she wanted.

Ingrid shouted that she was wet.

"An' A'm freezen."

She heard footsteps and two voices talking at the same time. The first one repeated the question.

"A'm looken f'r my Alexander."

"Your nationality?"

"Norwegian."

"And Alexander is?"

"Russian . . ."

"Status?"

"Hva?"

"Are you married?"

"Erm . . . ya."

"No Russians here now. They've been sent home."

"No, the' haven't, not all of 'em," Ingrid shouted.

"You have to wait for Protocol," said the voice after a short pause, and the hatch slammed shut again.

Ingrid wanted to scream that all this wasn't necessary; for this was the turning point, wasn't it?

But one side of the gate opened, there was the sound of an engine, a lorry rumbled out with a pile of wooden crates on top and drove off in the direction of the main road. Ingrid ran forward and was inside the gate before it slammed shut and was immediately surrounded by three uniformed men she hadn't seen. One grabbed her arm, but let go when he saw Kaja, and said that civilians were not permitted inside.

Ingrid was about to say that they'd better let her out again then, but a door in the shed to the left of the gate opened and a young, fair-haired man in shirtsleeves came out, he too was a soldier, he scrutinised her and asked if she was the person looking for a Russian.

Ingrid nodded.

He told her to accompany him inside and pointed to a spindle-back chair beside a cold stove. Ingrid watched him sit down behind a desk, pull open a drawer and lift out a book the size of a newspaper, which he opened and began to read from, using a ruler which he slowly moved down line by line with his fingertips. She had to show I.D., he said, without looking up.

"Hva?"

"I.D.?"

"Hva?" Ingrid repeated.

He eyed her.

"You don't have papers?"

Ingrid shook her head. He got up, walked around the desk and scrutinised both her and Kaja with interest.

"Well, you're a fine one, you are."

Ingrid unwrapped Kaja and held her up to her face to feel her warmth. He walked back to the desk and asked if she at least had a name, wrote it down, together with her date of birth and address, and said without looking up that it might take half an hour.

And this is the only concrete proof that Ingrid Marie Barrøy was in Sonderlager Mysen in the summer of 1946, her name, date of birth and address, entered in block letters into a historical document in the making, and countersigned by a woman, as procedures demanded, but without anyone else showing any subsequent interest, neither historians nor laymen, she is just one of 4,322 faceless names in these records, which incidentally didn't include a column to describe the purpose of the many visits.

Protocol turned out to be the nickname of a large woman in her fifties with barrel-shaped lower legs stuffed into beige shoes with shiny buckles, which were far too small for her. She was responsible for the female contingent of captives, whom she called alternately prisoners and internees, in a voice that was clearly used to being listened to by large groups of people. She was dressed in an outfit that looked like a combination of two uniforms, a nurse's and a soldier's, and over her shoulders she wore a cardigan with the sleeves hanging loose, while two coppery brown plaits were wound around her head so tightly that they resembled the brim of a hat. Her eyes were small, blue and smiling, and she looked almost disappointed when she heard that the visitor was searching for a *man*, but said Ingrid would still have to open her rucksack, no weapons, alcohol or medicines were allowed through these gates, you see.

Ingrid did as she was bidden, and Protocol immediately confiscated her knife.

"And what do you call this?"

Ingrid said it was her father's knife, she used it to cut bread.

Protocol put it in a locker mounted on the wall beside the stove. She also evinced an interest in Herman Vollheim's watch, pulled out the winder above the figure twelve and turned it back three minutes to set it by her own wristwatch, which was as big as a man's. Then she held up the metal cylinder that Henrik had sneaked into her rucksack and asked her to open it.

"A roll of film. You're not allowed to take photographs here."

Ingrid remembered that she had seen a camera in one of the rooms at Brynet, the one where she had the strange sensations, it was mounted on a collapsible stand leaning against the wall in the corner behind the door.

"But no camera, as far as I can see?" Protocol said, and placed the cylinder beside the knife in the locker. She said Ingrid should pack her rucksack again herself, waited until she had finished and strode ahead of her out of the door.

They walked in single file through a concentration camp in peacetime, a filtration camp and sorting machine of human shadows waking up to a new day and creeping out of barrack huts which bore white signs: *Warszawa, Gdynia, Vilno, Lwow, Poznan* ... a German concentration camp in the realm of peace, men and women and children kept in storage like shoes and hats in boxes, hay in a barn.

They weren't emaciated or apathetic like the Russian prisoners Ingrid had seen in the north during the war, but clad in ragged, grey sobriety, ex-soldiers, P.O.W.s, deserters, slaves, collaborators, sinners and victims, all jumbled in a border-breaking, stateless disarray, and who now reluctantly formed two lines along a main thoroughfare which the white sun was striving to transform from mud to dust.

"They're well looked after here," Protocol said over her shoulder. "They get food and water and clothes. The ones we trust are also given work and two kroner a week."

Ingrid whispered: "Ar the' given a bath too?"

"When the locals let them. They don't like Poles."

It seemed as though Our Lord had divided the war into two parts and then carved the carcass into human-like entities and mixed them all up in a barbed-wire basket. Now the silence gave way to Protocol's commanding figure, her fat fingers wrapped around a bunch of keys dangling from her skirt belt. Ingrid whispered:

"This hier's not reet."

"What's not right?" Protocol said.

Ingrid was watching a wide-eyed, grey-clad boy, on whose head rested a broad hand that looked like a cap, it had to be his father's hand, *he* was looking straight at her, too. Next to them stood another man with his hand on the shoulder of a girl in a faded, red-and-blue striped dress and knee-socks concertinaed above a pair of black clogs, their tips worn white. Next to them again stood a woman, and a slightly smaller woman, presumably mother and daughter, in dresses so alike that the signs of wear on one seemed to be a carbon copy of the other. After that, fifteen men of all ages and sizes with more or less shaven heads beside a man with grey hair and a full black beard sitting on a chair – they looked at Ingrid without batting an eyelid. Six men were standing in line under the *Gdynia* sign, to the right of them an old man sat on the ground, he too had a hand on his shoulder, it must have been his son's, a good-looking, erect, lean athlete staring straight ahead with what appeared to be a sneer on his face, and beside them, a smaller man, bare-chested with a stomach like an empty sack flopping over his belt and a solemnity in his eyes that contrasted with his friend's sneer, in his hand a cigarette, which he put to his lips and held there in the time it took for Ingrid to transfer her gaze to a woman of her own age, on her haunches with her back to Ingrid, humming into a wooden box on wheels that must have been a pram, and behind her a young man who raised his left hand to make a sign, beside a comrade who raised his right hand to pull the sign down again.

"You might be lucky," Protocol said. "Most of the people here are Poles, but we think there are still a few Russians hiding among them – of your age."

Ingrid mumbled that he wasn't her age.

Protocol turned and studied her.

"He's quait a bit younger," Ingrid said and noticed that the stiffness wouldn't leave her face. Protocol stared intently with small, squinting eyes and suddenly placed a hand on Ingrid's cheek, withdrew it and walked on and said loudly through the thinning crowd, her eyes fixed ahead, that lies got you nowhere, only the truth counted here.

"Look around you," she shouted. "They're here because they're lying about where they come from. They're lying about who they are and what they've done. They don't have an identity, they don't have names or papers and they claim they no longer have a country to return to, so what are we supposed to do with them?"

They had stopped in front of five men standing in a circle around a sixth who was sitting on the ground looking up at them. The formation was like a star which began to rearrange itself into a kind of line, and Protocol said something in a language Ingrid thought she recognised.

The men nodded, held their hands behind their backs and avoided looking at the intruders as far as possible.

"Russians, if you ask me," Protocol said. "They know all about Stalin's decree and insist he'll execute them if they travel back. They're Vlasov soldiers, I reckon. Can you see your man here?"

Ingrid ran her eyes along the line and whispered, no, and again, no, and glanced down at the figure sitting cross-legged on the ground, a barefoot man in his early twenties, the youngest of them, he grinned up at her, revealing black teeth.

"A smart alec, that one," Protocol said. "He's the one who's put ideas into the others' heads and got them to claim they're Poles."

She turned to one of them: "That one there says he's a Serb. But the Poles don't want anything to do with any of them."

"Can thas all speak Norwegian?" Ingrid said.

"He can," Protocol said, in the direction of the man on the ground. He rocked his head from side to side as though to suggest he might know something, it seemed to depend on the price, and Ingrid asked him if he had heard the name Alexander Nizhnikov. From Leningrad, about twenty-four years old.

His smile was reminiscent of a scar, he gazed up at his comrades and said something, it sounded like an order, they shook their heads and again they avoided looking at the two women as far as they possibly could.

"Yes, well, that was a shot in the dark," Protocol said, not overly disappointed, then changed her tone and said loudly: "Have you lot had any food?"

The five men standing said yes and the man on the ground said "*da, spasiba*", guffawed and added something Protocol didn't understand.

"Now he's talking Russian and Polish at the same time, would you believe it?"

Ingrid wasn't spared the sound of jangling keys, but caught sight of a young couple standing between the last two huts talking to each other in subdued voices, the woman in a faded, striped dress with loose threads hanging from the waistband, a green, buttonless cardigan which she held together with crossed arms, while he wore the same indefinable grey material as the others, but with a threadbare suit jacket and a loosely knotted tie, the end of which he had tucked between two buttons in a creased ochre shirt. Protocol had followed her gaze.

"Yes, a special pair, they are. Go and have a word with them." Ingrid looked at her askance. "Yes, go on. They've been here for more than a year. He's Polish and doesn't want to go home. She doesn't want to go home either, even though she's Norwegian. It's love, they say. Love, my foot. But they're tough 'uns, I'll give them that."

33

Ingrid stopped two to three metres away. The woman glanced over at her with a wary smile while the man stared into the forests on the other side of the barbed wire, stuffed a hand into his pocket and half-turned, with the result that Ingrid saw him in profile. She shouted that her name was Ingrid and asked if she could have a word with them. The woman came closer.

"Are you Norwegian?"

Ingrid was Norwegian. "My goodness, what are you doing here?"

Ingrid launched into her story again, now for the first time with a sense that it was being listened to with due attention, that it was credible, as though she had finally met the right person to tell it to. But the moment she felt this, she was unable to carry on.

The woman came even closer and took her by the arm.

"There, there."

The man put a hand to his forehead and turned to face them. Ingrid buried her face in Kaja's hair and saw him whisper something to the woman before leaving them and sloping off between the huts.

"He's shy," the woman said, and told her that she was teaching him Norwegian. She said her name was Kari and placed a hand on Kaja's head while continuing to tell Ingrid about her situation, as though she felt the same urgency to unburden herself. Ingrid stared at her expectantly, but nothing happened when Kari's eyes met Kaja's. Ingrid said that she had hoped to find her child's father here.

The woman went on to talk about her husband, about how he had been taken prisoner by the Germans soon after they occupied Poland in 1939, how he had survived various hard labour camps in Germany and Norway since then, but he doesn't want to talk about them, not even to me, she said in lilting tones resonant of Herman Vollheim's accent.

Ingrid put the rucksack down onto the drying mud and asked if Kari would mind holding Kaja for her.

"Not at all. What's the matter?"

"A 'ave t' sit down f'r a bit."

Ingrid slumped to the ground and glanced over at Protocol and the six Russians, who appeared to be engaged in a normal conversation, there was even some laughter, and behind them the grey wall of silent, human-like figures beneath a sun that came and went again, Ingrid blinked.

Kari sat down beside her and held Kaja on her lap. There was more dirt than grass. Ingrid pulled up a few blades, one by one, and laid them in a pile while Kari explained how she had allowed herself to be locked up to get her husband out, she laughed at that.

"Tha's laik me," Ingrid said.

Without taking her eyes off Kaja, Kari said that she didn't think so, she didn't know anyone like herself. Ingrid thought the same about herself, and asked if she wasn't allowed to marry the man?

"We *are* married. But they won't give him papers simply on those grounds."

Ingrid asked how long she was intending to stay.

"As long as it takes."

"Tha's like me," Ingrid repeated.

"I don't think so," Kari repeated, and Ingrid said she felt better now, she'd had a feeling that her Alexander was hiding somewhere in the crowd here, that he was watching her, she had felt this for weeks, his eyes behind trees and people and railway carriages, urging her on, a feeling that was beginning to fade as she sat here, and that was the complete opposite of how it should be.

Kari peered at her quizzically and said she must not give up.

Ingrid gazed at her.

Kari whispered to the ground:

"There are more Russians here than the handful over there. I can get Czek to talk to them. He can speak Russian, but it might take a while."

Ingrid asked why.

"It's hard."

"Hva's hard?"

"He's the leader of the Poles, but he also has some friends among the Russians. But go and ask Protocol if you can stay here a few days. Say you haven't got any papers, money, anything, say you can sleep in *Gdynia* with me, we know each other and you've come to persuade me to go home ..."

Ingrid saw that Protocol had left the six men, who were all now sitting on the ground in a circle, around what looked like a game.

"A can't do that."

"What can't you do?"

"A can't bi hier."

Kari fixed her with a stare, took off her headscarf, smoothed it out, folded it and tied it around her head again. Ingrid asked when she had last spoken to anyone outside. Kari didn't answer. Ingrid guessed she was around nineteen, maybe twenty years old, and said she should just keep talking, Ingrid couldn't get up anyway. And all the time her husband stood between the huts watching them, Kari talking non-stop and Ingrid listening, the complete opposite of how it should have been, as their fingers played with Kaja, who laughed.

34

Ingrid Marie Barrøy spent the next few days in a very small room in a nearby boarding house, intensely preoccupied with what had happened when she was in the camp. All the days were long and alike, and the weather was always the same, an invisible mildewy rain at night and an unbearable heat during the day.

Food was provided in the boarding house, and she was able to wash her clothes cheaply in a machine. She consulted the *Rutebok* to find a way home, the right way. She wrote a letter to Suzanne telling her what she thought this stepdaughter of hers needed to know about her comings and goings, it had been a short journey, and she would soon be home again, maybe even before Suzanne received the letter, she missed them, she missed the distant continent called Barrøy, and Suzanne too, will tha greet t' others.

But Ingrid didn't leave.

What about a letter to Henrik at Brynet? Now in the clear light of day. She wrote it, too, but never sent it. Also she considered sending a letter to Mariann Vollheim, but didn't even write that one.

She wandered around in a village with low timber houses and tall trees, small gardens full of ripe fruit and berries and dogs that were chained up but didn't bark. Every day she walked around the camp once, twice, three times, closing in on it as if it were prey, and – as she passed a photography shop – was reminded of the roll of film Protocol had given back to her, together with the knife, when she left the camp.

She opened the door to the shop, went in and told a man behind a black counter who didn't get up from the chair he was sitting on that she would like to have it developed.

He grabbed the roll and looked at it:

"Ah, a twelver. Right."

Ingrid cast her eye around the strange room, so much like the studio she had been photographed in during the war, with a doctor who had cured her. She asked if the man was a photographer.

"Don't I look like one, then?"

Ingrid had no answer; she asked how long it would take.

"To be photographed?" He sucked his teeth, snapped his fingers and smiled with his blue eyes beneath thick, blond brows which met in a tuft above the broad bridge of his nose.

Ingrid said she meant for the film to be developed.

"Might well take a week or two, I would think."

"Hvafor?"

"Hvafor what?" he mimicked, and, slowly, Ingrid asked why it would take so long to develop a film.

He said that was the time it took, handed her a slip of paper on which he had just jotted something down on and torn off a yellow envelope in which he had placed the roll of film. Ingrid read what was on the paper and saw a date at the end of the month.

She asked what it would cost to be photographed with Kaja?

He came around the counter, stopped and looked at them, his chin in his left hand and his right hand under his elbow, and named an amount that caused Ingrid to bridle. Kaja smiled at him. He pointed a playful finger at her. Ingrid said they would have to wait then, and left.

Back at the boarding house, she went in to see the couple who ran the place and said that she would like to stay a few more days, but didn't have the money, could she clean the rooms for them, or cook or do some gardening, in exchange for board and lodging?

The man sent his wife a questioning look. She turned to Ingrid and said, yes, they could probably sort something out.

Ingrid went over and gave her a hug, both of them blushed, then she hurried up to her room and locked the door behind her, there were locks on all the doors in this house, and hardly any guests.

The next day, too, Ingrid walked around the camp twice and tried to pick out Kari and her husband through the barbed wire, but only recognised the six Russians, who again were sitting in a circle in the dirt, bent over their game. They didn't seem to notice her. After that, she went to see the photographer, who was flabbergasted and said that it was far too soon, couldn't Ingrid read? Didn't he develop the films himself, Ingrid asked. He mimicked her again and said, indeed he did, but his laboratory assistant was on holiday at the moment, was there anything else?

In the afternoon Ingrid cleaned the only room that had been rented out for the previous two nights, while the woman of the house stood in the doorway, arms folded, watching her, and remarked:

"It's strange not having anything to do."

They laughed at that.

Ingrid changed the beds and washed the stairs, and in the evening she had dinner with the couple. They had lived in the same house since they got married fifty-three years before, and had no children, but on the wall Ingrid could see their wedding photograph.

Ingrid hadn't explained why she was there. She did so now, but didn't tell them much about the journey, and they looked at her sympathetically.

The woman was called Evy, and she said that Ingrid was plucky.

"Yes, you can say that again," said her husband, whose name was Jonas. Both of them looked as though they were talking just to have something to say, like so many others Ingrid had met, with the exception of Kari, there was something about Kari. Then he said:

"Let's not talk any more about this now."

Ingrid looked at him in puzzlement, then fed Kaja. Evy, too, said Kaja was a beautiful child. On that, at least, they all saw eye to eye. Would Ingrid like some more coffee?

Ingrid said, yes, please.

Jonas said:

"If only we could get rid of this cursed camp, so we could see something of the trotting track at long last."

"We agreed not to talk about that," Evy said.

"Mm, that's right," Jonas said.

When Ingrid was in the camp, Kari had told her that she had first set eyes on Czek, as she called him, behind the barbed-wire fence in a camp outside the village where she went to school. She had known there and then – without a shadow of doubt in her mind – that there goes my future husband. She had even said this out loud, and a local who was passing by had glared at her strangely and asked if she was mad. Subsequently, she had smuggled food into the camp and had got to know him better, and become more and more convinced that she was right. And the whole time it seemed as though Kari was trying hard not to speak her own dialect, as if she was practising to be someone else.

Ingrid had repeated that Kari was like her, and had reflected that if there was anything that set them apart it was that one of them had a husband and the other a child, but both of them lacked a vital element in their lives.

The following day, she walked around the camp once again, spotted Kari and waved to her. Kari came up to the fence and stood there smiling, raised her hand to wave to Kaja, and said to Ingrid through the barbed wire, in the same soft tone as when she had asked whether she was Norwegian:

"Are you still here?"

Ingrid said she would be back, but realised her voice didn't carry. She presumed this was because of the fence, not the distance. Kari tilted her head and smiled, and Ingrid cast down her eyes, turned and walked on with a feeling of deep betrayal.

35

O n her way back to the boarding house she called in at the photographer's once again. And the day after that. And the fourth and the fifth day, and the photographer always said the same, as though he had fallen into some kind of resigned routine, but on the sixth day a yellow envelope lay on his black counter, waiting for her.

"Thirteen by eighteen. Yes," he said.

Ingrid paid an exorbitant sum, took the envelope back to her room, opened it and found twelve prints, one of which was completely black, together with an equal number of negatives in a separate sleeve.

She spread out the prints on the table by the window. Eleven snaps depicting either one or two men. At first she didn't recognise either of them. But in one photograph the two men were sitting next to each other, in an armchair, she recognised the room as the parlour at Brynet, with the open fireplace in the background. Between them stood a low table with a bottle of spirits on it, together with two glasses and an ashtray containing a pipe and what looked like a cigar. They looked as if they were celebrating something and closely related, one of them had gloves on both hands, the other wore only one, the same type of glove, and both men sported a thick, black beard and had bristly hair that was five or six centimetres long, one of them was greying, the other black-haired. She recognised Henrik first, but put two fingers over the face of the man at his side, so the beard and hair were hidden and only the eyes were visible, and saw a young man, Alexander Nizhnikov, whom she had shaved and whose hair she had cut around the time they lay together in the North Chamber on Barrøy, as though he were a prisoner in her house, too, whereas here he was enjoying unbounded freedom on a farm in the Norwegian mountains, in the company of another soldier, they had let their hair and beards grow, and both were smiling.

In three of the photographs the young man was on the slope leading down to the mill and sauna, in deep snow, wearing Norwegian breeches, cardigan and woollen cap, with thick mittens on his hands. He was on skis. In another he was lying in a snowdrift laughing at the photographer, obviously after a fall. In a third he was on his knees in snow to his waist, bare-headed and flashing that same white smile, a few logs of wood resting on the arm with the gloved hand, while he held up two of the fingers on the other, making an amputated V-sign, the same way Ingrid had seen Winston Churchill doing in news-papers.

There was also a photograph taken in the wash room with the three sinks, where he was standing half-naked and clearly being teased about something he also thought was funny, by the photographer, Henrik, presumably. In the next three snaps the two men were posing next to each other in two different rooms, in the first they were in the kitchen at Brynet. But there was too much back light, which obscured their faces. And the two other photographs were taken in the room with the blackout blinds, against some shelves full of books lying flat, Henrik with a release cord hanging from his undamaged hand. Ingrid noticed that Alexander was taller than him, and both of them were laughing at the camera again, a little differently in the two photographs, as if they had been taken immediately after each other, the first before their smiles were at their broadest, and the second shortly afterwards.

In the last snapshot Alexander was sitting in the chair Henrik had been sitting in when he had had the talk with her.

He was engrossed in a book, at ease, his profile as if hewn from one white and one black block of marble and joined seamlessly, his eyes were half in shadow. Ingrid stared for so long she thought she was going mad, and there was nothing she could do about it.

She showed the pictures to Kaja, who attempted to tear them to shreds. Ingrid looked at them again, put them in a pile, shuffled them and spread them across the table again to find the one point she must have missed – Ingrid who always missed something – in these static glimpses of the irrevocable. And she continued to do so until she could no longer see, as darkness had fallen outside the narrow, curtainless window, by which time Kaja had cried herself to sleep without Ingrid even noticing.

36

Ingrid got up as if on autopilot. Herman Vollheim's watch showed a quarter past seven, she changed Kaja without waking her up, dressed herself and Kaja and went down to the kitchen, which was empty. She made breakfast in the way she had seen Evy do, coffee, porridge and syrup and three slices of bread for Jonas and one for Evy and two for herself and one for Kaja, which she cut into cubes. They sat waiting.

Evy came down in a tent-like shift, through which Ingrid could make out her figure against the light from the open door, and said in a sleepy voice that Ingrid was a quick learner, maybe they should fry some eggs?

Ingrid placed a frying pan on the stove, added a knob of margarine, and Jonas came down in worn slippers, blue checked pyjamas, as always when they had no guests, and peered down at Kaja, who was sitting on the floor, and said, crikey, he had never smiled at such a sweet girl so early in the morning.

Evy said that he never smiled, full stop, then turned to Ingrid and told her she'd like some cranberry jam on her porridge, explained where it was in the cupboard, as though that were at all necessary, and Ingrid fried three eggs feeling she was still on autopilot.

They ate in silence like three lodgers.

Ingrid cleared the table, washed up and went out at half past eight.

It wasn't the small hatch in the camp gate that opened this time, but the door at the side. The upper part of Protocol's body leaned out, she rolled her eyes heavenward and asked irritably what she wanted now?

Ingrid said she wanted to talk to Kari. And that she didn't have her rucksack with her today, only the child.

"I can see that," Protocol said. "What do you want to see her about?"

Ingrid didn't answer.

Protocol shrugged and opened the gate. Ingrid thanked her.

"V.I.P!," Protocol shouted to a man half in uniform who was eyeing them from the door of the guard hut. Protocol frisked her from top to toe, nodded and let her pass.

Ingrid began to walk down between the barrack huts, enveloped in the same silence as before, but thought she discerned more dignity and defiance in these eyes which had become a week older now, these figures standing still, each in their own cage, waiting for someone to come and set their clocks going again.

She caught sight of Kari and her husband, who this time too

were whispering to each other a good distance away from the other human shadows.

"I knew it," Kari said cheerily, when she noticed Ingrid, and looked as though she were about to clap her hands.

"No, tha didn't," Ingrid said, and stopped. Czeslaw gave a sheepish smile. Ingrid said she had brought some photographs along. Kari said:

"Oh, yes. Shall we go over there?"

They went to the fence, Czeslaw followed and halted five metres away, like a sentry. Ingrid gave Kari the envelope, she opened it and looked at the photographs one by one without saying a word, but stared for a long time at the last, in which Alexander was sitting in the armchair reading, where he was most like himself, despite his beard and dishevelled hair, and even though his eyes were in the shade.

"I presume that's him?"

"Yes."

"Who's the other one?"

Ingrid told her about Henrik, the partisan. Kari nodded slowly and held the photograph in the air as a sign to Czeslaw to come closer. Today, too, he was wearing the shabby suit jacket and ochre shirt, but now his tie was hanging loose and dangling over his emaciated stomach. He examined the photograph and shook his head. Kari said something Ingrid didn't understand. Czeslaw looked as though he had been asked to do something he was reluctant to comply with. He reflected, examined the picture again, turned to Ingrid and said in broken Norwegian that she should let him keep it and come back tomorrow.

Ingrid tried to give him a hug. He kept her at an arm's length and said that he couldn't be of any help, he was quite sure of that, all he could do was *try*. Ingrid gave Kari a hug instead, then hurried out of the camp without looking at a single face.

Next morning she was there again, this time pushing an old, unused pram adorned with blue flowers, which Evy and Jonas had kept in a shed in the garden because they didn't have the heart to throw it out. But Kaja wasn't in the pram, it was full of jars of jam that Ingrid had been allowed to gather from the cellar in the boarding house, strawberry, raspberry, redcurrant, gooseberry, from before the war, Evy must have held them in reserve during the war years, and there was no need for them anymore. Protocol opened the gate and rolled her eyes heavenward again, and said it was Sunday, was Ingrid thinking of going to Mass?

She didn't understand.

"They're so religious, they are. There are three priests here. They take it in turns and they also divvy up the Absolution."

Ingrid pushed the pram in through the gate, as though she had already been given permission to enter. Protocol peered down into it.

"Bribes, that's what we like."

They attempted a smile at each other.

"I suppose you want to talk to Kari again?"

Ingrid nodded. "On your way then. I'll see to this lot."

The sound of hymns being sung could be heard from several of the huts. Outside *Warszawa*, people were standing with their backs turned, as if they were waiting to go into a building where there was no room for them, and were all mumbling at the same time, like a low-pitched choir.

Ingrid couldn't find either Kari or her husband, and walked on to the patch of land at the end of the camp, from which only the barbed wire and the motionless forests were to be seen. She waited. Just a few days before she had been on the other side of this fence looking in, when Kari was standing where Ingrid was now, and she could feel the sisterhood between them; and when she had shown her the photographs Ingrid had also understood why. And now she didn't dare to turn around to see whether anyone was watching her.

Ingrid had brought the woollen blankets with her. She spread them out on the ground, sat down and sang and played with Kaja, who played with Bonken, until Kari came and stood in the sunshine in front of them, wearing the same tatty dress, which looked as though she had washed it, and a white pinafore, it was Sunday, and Ingrid was in Mariann's dress, which she had also just washed. She squinted up at Kari in the sun, and said she was going to spend some of her last money on clothes for Kaja, what did Kari think about that?

Kari thought she should.

She sat down, gave Ingrid the photograph back and said she should go with Czek now while the service was on.

"The Russians aren't Catholics," she said, as if this made any sense.

Ingrid spotted Czeslaw by the closest hut, motioned to Kari to take care of Kaja, got to her feet and walked slowly towards him. He turned and began to walk away before she could reach him. Ingrid speeded up with the result that they arrived at the rear door of the *Tobruk* hut at the same time. He faced her and murmured that someone by the name of Pavel had said he was willing to talk to her, he's actually a Russian and called something else, but he speaks such good Polish that no-one has the slightest suspicion, he also speaks Norwegian.

Ingrid nodded.

"He's been here for over a year."

Ingrid nodded again.

"Like us."

Ingrid nodded a third time.

Czeslaw opened the door, let her in and closed it behind her.

Ingrid found herself in a dark passageway, the first door on the left was open. She entered a narrow room with three levels of bunk beds on each side and a small window at the same height above the floor as the hatch in the main gate, a white ace of diamonds above a table which in fact was no more than a stool, with a candlestick on it. All the beds were made, pillowless and unoccupied, except for the lowest one on the left, where a young man sat looking at her.

She thought she recognised his gaze from her first experience of running the gauntlet through the camp. He blinked his long, dark eyelashes and nodded in the direction of the bunk opposite. Ingrid sat down. His eyes lowered and fixed themselves on the photograph she was holding between her fingers. She was about to give it to him, but he shook his head and said with a faraway smile:

"Sasha."

"Yes," Ingrid said.

"He left with the others last year. He went home to Leningrad and his Maria. He couldn't live without her."

Ingrid said Alexander had once written *her* a letter, in which he expressed his love for *her*.

Pavel smiled.

"I've also loved many girls. But none of them is here any longer. My family in Minsk has gone. We're not Russians, we were Jews, now I'm a Catholic."

Ingrid looked down at the photograph, which became clearer as the light from the ace of diamonds in the wall became brighter. In the candlestick on the stool was a burned-out Paschal candle, which someone had carved with a knife.

"We played chess," he said. "The first time at Litsa. We were taken prisoner only a few days apart, but ended up the following autumn in the same camp at Rognan. We built roads. And railways. Most of us starved to death or were killed. Eighteen months later only he and I were left. We sang 'Kakhovka' in our hearts and played chess."

He had slender, feminine hands with short, manicured nails, and moved them as if he were playing a delicate instrument.

"Sasha was sent to the coast and spent a few months in a camp at a place called . . . I can't remember. It was there he was put on board the *Rigel* . . . He said there must have been three or four thousand men, mostly Russians. While I myself was marched in a column over the mountains and put on a train and sent here, by which time there was peace. Shortly afterwards, he arrived here too, we thought we were seeing ghosts, we played chess here as well."

"Hvo won?" Ingrid said, her eyes fixed on the candle.

He smiled.

"Me, as a rule. In Rognan we chewed bread until it was like dough, then shaped it into chess-pieces, played a few games, then ate them. Here we were able to make pieces out of clay. We didn't need to eat them, we're all right here. After the Russians were sent home, we even got some proper pieces, from the locals, but there's nobody here anymore who's very good at chess. He was like a brother to me."

Pavel's head was shaven, and a number of white scars criss-crossed his scalp, the result of a Norwegian guard's failed attempt to kill him with a spade, they resembled misshapen letters of the alphabet. His features were pronounced and handsome, his eyes clear, and he had almost no facial hair.

Ingrid asked how Alexander had got here from Brynet.

"On foot. But the war was over by then and he was given food and help. It was an easy trip compared with the one the previous winter. He couldn't do much with his hands, of course, but he worked for a week in a laundry, he also helped a baker, then he took a bus the last part of the way and arrived here alone at the end of May, by which time there were over a hundred thousand Russians in the country . . ."

"So hvafor didn't tha go with 'im hvan he went heim?"

He looked at her again:

"Stalin doesn't like Jews or Poles, and my life as a Pole had already begun on the road from Rognan. I wondered for a while whether to become a Serb, but they were treated just as badly as the Russians, and my Norwegian wasn't good enough then. Today I could probably pass as a Norwegian, don't you think?"

Ingrid smiled and said yes.

"So you and I could get married and I could get my I.D. papers?"

Ingrid laughed.

"I was only joking," he said.

"A know," Ingrid said.

He looked up at the light coming in.

"Protocol teaches me Norwegian in secret. That's my only hope."

Ingrid nodded.

He asked to see the photograph one more time.

She gave it to him.

He sat studying it. Ingrid fidgeted uneasily. She was sitting on some coarse, grey wool, which was wrapped around the mattress with the same tight precision as at the hospital where she had been admitted during the war. Now she wrapped the blankets in the same way on Barrøy. She had pressed the palms of her hands down into the mattress on either side of her thighs, and locked her fingers around the edge. She noticed that her knuckles were white. She loosened her grip and raised her left hand to check that it was still there, tightened her grip again and kept on staring at a foreign man studying a photograph of her man.

Suddenly she announced to the cramped room that she hadn't been able to trust anyone along the way, nobody would tell her the truth.

Pavel looked up, his eyes moist. Ingrid realised her own were dry, and that her grip on the mattress had not relaxed, her feet were placed neatly together in someone else's shoes on a sand-scoured floor.

"You might well be right about that," he said, and gave her back the photograph.

She asked if he wanted to keep it, she had something they called negatives.

"No, that would weaken my resolve," he said. "And I need to be strong."

Ingrid asked him what *he* wasn't telling her.

He turned this over in his mind, gave a fleeting smile, and said he missed her dialect, it was all he missed from Rognan, there were some good Norwegian people in those parts, too, and he would never forget them.

Ingrid said she wasn't from Rognan and repeated her question.

"Alexander's a Jew, too," he said at length. "But he's not religious, doesn't go to the synagogue and never prays. He sees himself as a Russian, through and through, and a proud Russian at that."

Ingrid took a deep breath and asked what that had to do with anything.

"Sooner or later someone might find out. And it's not we who decide who we are."

Ingrid asked again what that had to do with anything.

He looked away and said:

"He's got a son."

"Oh, yes?"

Pavel went on:

"Maria was pregnant when he was called up. He received a letter at Litsa telling him that it was a boy, whom she'd named after him. He was nineteen, she was seventeen. But he never told anyone about his son, for fear that even mentioning his name might bring a curse down on them ..."

"But he did tell *tha*?"

"Yes, he was ill at one point and thought he was going to die, so I was to . . ."

Ingrid looked down at someone else's shoes on her feet and said, so there wasn't any curse then, he survived, didn't he?

Pavel didn't answer.

She wanted to ask if Alexander had ever mentioned *her* or if he had said anything about Mariann. She wanted to ask if Pavel knew anything about Alexander's family, his parents and any brothers and sisters he might have, so this could be noted down in her sketch pad next to the bus and train times and place names and fragments of all those things that were impossible to comprehend in the year 1946. She wanted to ask whether he would like to see Kaja, but knew what the answer would be, that he had to be strong.

But she could still move all her limbs, so she quickly looked up at the ace of diamonds and down at this man with the terrible scars on his skull, a man who had no idea who she was, but had answered the vital question and enabled her to reach the decisive turning point. She leaned forward and wanted to touch the scars with her fingertips. But her hands were locked around the mattress. She released them, one finger at a time, and got to her feet so that she could look him in the eye when she shook his hand and thanked him. Pavel remained seated, and Ingrid walked out into the sunshine with the photograph.

*

Kari looked up at her expectantly and asked how it had gone. Czeslaw stood by the fence, the sentry, one hand in his pocket and his tie hanging over his shoulder. There was a slight wind, but there was no sound in the trees. Ingrid said that it had gone well and sat down and laid her right hand upside down on the blanket so that Kaja could wriggle onto it, it was a game they played. Czeslaw walked slowly past them and in between the huts, where, today too, the Russians sat hunched over their game.

"Tha's expecten'," Ingrid said.

Kari glanced around her and asked in a whisper how on earth Ingrid could know, it didn't show yet.

Ingrid smiled.

"An' tha's a little sister now," she mumbled to the back of her daughter's head. Kaja was trying to keep her balance on Ingrid's hand.

Kari repeated her question, how could she see?

Ingrid shrugged and said she wanted to give her something in return for her help, and dug out Herman Vollheim's watch.

"I can't accept this," Kari said, as the lid sprang open between her fingers and the hands moved in the light of day and were black against the gilt Roman numerals. Ingrid said, yes, it's a fine watch, but she didn't need it any longer. Kari hesitated.

"You can sell it," she suggested. "So you can get some money to travel home."

"A have money."

"No, you haven't."

Ingrid couldn't remember exactly what she had told Kari. She said she had agreed to do the cleaning in the boarding house for a week or two, for payment, and that Kari could keep the watch until that time was over, it has to be wound every morning.

"Not in the evening?"

"No, in th' mornin'."

"No, I can't take it," Kari said.

Ingrid got up and took Kaja in her arms, stood watching as Kari shook and folded the blankets, answered, yes, to Kari's question about whether she should carry them over to the gate for her. Ingrid waved to Czeslaw, who nodded solemnly back. The church service was over, the human shadows filed out into the daylight. By the guard hut the empty pram was waiting for them. Protocol was nowhere to be seen. Ingrid told Kari she would come and say goodbye before she left, put the blankets in the pram, sat Kaja on top of them and wheeled it out of the gate, which was opened by the man who had let her in on the first day.

37

Ingrid lay in bed in her room at the boarding house in the south of the country, thinking about her father, whom she hadn't been able to picture for the whole of the journey. Hans Barrøy and his indomitable life, which was extinguished like a candle in a sudden storm, now she could see him again.

Downstairs she heard Evy and Jonas' footsteps, they were finishing off for the day, they closed the windows on the ground floor, threw the rubbish in the bin by the gate, put out some milk for the cat, Jonas switched off the lights in the same order as always, his slippers scuffing on the staircase, the gentle opening and closing of the bedroom door, anxious not to wake Ingrid and Kaja. Then Evy's tiptoeing up the same staircase, another light switch turned off, the bathroom door opening and the subsequent sound of running water in the taps and pipes. Ingrid got out of bed and threw on a dressing gown, one she had borrowed from Jonas, and went into the corridor. Evy understood everything she whispered to her, switched the light back on and went down the stairs and into the reception area, where the telephone was.

*

Ingrid Marie Barrøy never went back to see Kari and Czeslaw Garbarek in Sonderlager Mysen. The very next morning one of Jonas' acquaintances, a butcher, drove her and Kaja in a lorry to Eidsvoll, he had to collect some animals there. Evy waved as they left, she had given them a freshly baked loaf for the journey, together with butter, jam, nine shiny apples and a kilo of boiled potatoes wrapped in newspaper.

When Ingrid got out at Eidsvoll railway station, the butcher gave her ten kroner and said it was from Jonas, but on no account was she to tell Evy. She was also given a few parting words of advice, which she didn't need, and noticed that it wasn't raining today either.

Inside the station building she was informed that the day train had departed, the next northbound one wouldn't be arriving until ten hours later, the night train. Ingrid had counted her money and knew how far it would take her. She bought a ticket to Trondheim, no, not via Røros, thank you. A new small piece of cardboard was put in her hand and she sat down on a comfortable wooden bench – there was nobody else in the waiting room – and began to study the *Rutebok*, while Kaja crawled around on the floor, black and white tiles, Ingrid thought it was dirty there, but didn't bother.

She left her rucksack with the official in the glass cage, went out and walked around the station. She wandered among the houses which, here too, were surrounded by trees that were taller than they were, past a school playground and saw that it was full of children on swings, playing hopscotch and running after large, brown balls, school had started again, it was plain to see, summer was over, even this one.

She trudged on and saw a bakery she had no need to enter, thanks to Evy. She thought about Evy, in some ways it makes no difference which end of the country you live.

She spotted a shop selling clothes, including children's, and decided she couldn't afford to buy everything she wanted for Kaja, if they were to make it all the way home.

She opened the door, went in and saw two young girls, identically dressed and with blond plaits, standing behind a counter that resembled a coffin, they looked like sisters. Behind them stood a woman of Ingrid's age, looking straight at her and smiling, while the girls nervously shuffled their feet. Ingrid bought what she thought Kaja needed. The girls squabbled about who was to crank the cash register, and who should put the money in the till and who should give Ingrid her change. Something had also to be written down, in two ledgers. Their mother said Ingrid had been wise to buy a bonnet for the child, to protect her from the sun. And none of them made fun of her dialect.

Ingrid got off the train in Trondheim, now firmly resolved to go into the town. She had seen the sun rise above the Dovrefjell mountains and had studied a street plan in the *Rutebok*, she had seen snow glistening on the mountaintops and felt a surprising sense of relief that none of the people she had met on her travels had told her more than they had and that she hadn't asked more than she had dared, as though the journey had been as good as it could have been, in retrospect, it was a relief that she hadn't found out more than she had, even Henrik's story about Alexander's hands had been bearable, but here, too, all her fantasies came to an end.

Now she walked into Trondheim with her ears closed and slavishly followed a street that was as straight as an arrow and which she had picked out on the map in the *Rutebok*. She made a sharp turn and continued along an equally straight street until she reached the town's famous cathedral, which she had heard about ever since she was a child. She walked around it and discovered that for once the trees were not as tall as the building, after which she returned the same way that she had come. And nobody stared at her. People didn't stare at one another either, as far as Ingrid could judge, but went about their business in the same purposeful, unruffled manner, as though the world were as it should be.

She didn't go into any shops, she looked at the displays in three windows though, a shoe shop, a hairdresser's and a bridal salon. In the latter there were three enormous mirrors with silver frames leaning against some black, wooden chairs arranged at an angle to one another, such that people – looking from outside – could see themselves from three different sides, only a view of them from behind was missing. And there wasn't a dress or a wedding veil to be seen.

Following the directions of two young boys, whom Ingrid talked to without any sense of shyness, she walked down to the harbour and strolled along the quays, asking people on fishing boats and freighters if they were going north, could they give her a lift, they could not.

She sat in the sun outside a storehouse and scraped off the black letters the newspaper had left on the potatoes, broke them into small pieces and gave Kaja as much as she wanted, of Evy's jam, too. She ate the rest of the potatoes herself, counted the clean nappies she had left and bought a bottle of milk in a shop next to a coal yard dominated by what looked like a tar-coated pyramid.

Early in the afternoon she was offered a lift on a northbound freighter, but no further than to a place called Bessaker, and the skipper didn't think this was a good idea, because from Bessaker there weren't many boats heading further north.

Ingrid said that didn't matter, the direction was as it should be.

She arrived in Bessaker in the middle of the night, was given permission by a stevedore to sleep in a crab factory canteen, washed her clothes and nappies in a hand basin and the very next evening was offered a lift on a fishing smack north to Rørvik, the place where she had once waited for the *Munkefjord*, which had taken her to Kongsmoen at the start of her journey.

Back then she had waited here for three days. Now she barely had time to buy milk and bread in the general store on the quay before she spotted a fishing cutter outside, which was being loaded with salt. She recognised the markings on the bow, the large N for Nordland, and ran out and shouted from the quayside that she wanted to go up north with them, this was no longer a question, these were her people.

"Hvor ar tha headen?" said the lad in a thick Icelandic sweater and clogs, who was down on the deck operating the hoist.

Ingrid said she was going to Innøyr.

"Ya, ya, it's on th' route. But we won't bi setten out til th' morrow."

Ingrid spent the night in the same shack as before. Kaja was sunburnt from her nose down, but her forehead was nice and white beneath a new bonnet – she hadn't cried one single time on the journey north, and didn't now, either.

At the crack of dawn next morning they boarded the cutter, which took more than twenty-four hours, and made three stops, to transport them to Innøyr in the north. Ingrid stood on the deck for most of the voyage, exchanging the occasional word with the lad and the skipper, taking in the fjords and islands and the familiar mountain contours which rose on the horizon ahead of them, listening to the cries of the gulls, breathing in the sea, there were only the four of them on board, and there was nothing to ask about and nothing to tell.

In Innøyr, too, she went into the shack where she had slept when she set out, and sat on a bench by the window staring at the cold stove and logs, and at the picture of King Håkon hanging above one of the bunk beds, everything had become cooler, clearer, and the sounds had returned. She had some bread and there was still a little of Evy's butter and jam left. And three apples. They ate, and she wondered whether they should spend the night here before she trekked over the mountains towards Malvika, suddenly it felt as if she were in an unnecessary hurry to get home.

But this was more of a pleasant thought than something that was actually feasible, so she tied Kaja to her belly, slung the rucksack over her shoulders and began to walk. Once again her step was light, though she was bent forward, as Kaja had become heavier, and the rucksack lighter. The sun was shining and there was a light breeze. On parts of the way she walked in the shadow of the mountains. They drank from every stream they crossed, she fed and changed Kaja, and hung the nappies from her rucksack to dry, and when she stood at the highest point of the pass Herman Vollheim's watch showed exactly six o'clock in the evening, she could see that, too, by the height of the sun shining high above her islands in the sea.

She sat gazing at the sight and listening before embarking upon the final descent, the only stage of the journey she had been accompanied by someone, apart from the short distance where Carl had led the way. The ferns now reached up to her waist and above, they had become limp and brown, *this* is where autumn begins.

She arrived in Malvika as the sun was sinking into the sea

and saw Daniel leading a horse into the stable. He didn't see her. She waited until he came out again, and when he finally caught sight of her he couldn't believe his eyes, he cackled like an idiot and ran past her and shouted in through the porch door – our Ingrid's come home!

Mathea came out and threw herself around Ingrid's neck and wept and held her at arm's length and stared at her in a way that made Ingrid think she must have changed, and not necessarily for the better.

"Well, A never. Come in, come in."

Ingrid went into the sumptuous house, which was nothing out of the ordinary now, but was as clean and bright as ever. She shook Adolf's hand, he too rose from his chair by the window with a tear in his eye. Fortunately, he noticed Kaja and managed to say:

"Bless my soul, my little lass, what lang locks tha's got."

Dinner was served, and Ingrid told them everything that could be told in a household like this, to a receptive audience, keeping as close to the truth as everyone else had done. They hadn't much to add, except for meaningful nods and a few "Would-you-believe-it?"s. Daniel, Liljan and Malin, the tenant farmer's daughter, were all present. Adolf said that Ingrid's cousin, Lars, had been over in the whaler and had asked about her, and Adolf had had to tell him what he knew about her plans. Lars said that in that case the færing could stay in Adolf's boathouse waiting for her.

Ingrid smiled and said as politely as possible that it was more likely that Lars had come to fetch the færing, yes, he had, but Adolf had refused to let him take it.

Adolf protested sheepishly while Mathea and Liljan set to work clearing the tables and washing up, and Kaja sat on Malin's lap, who looked as if she already lived in the house and was planning to carry on doing so. Ingrid turned to Daniel and asked, could he come to the island in the autumn and plough and harrow the last garden on Barrøy, which lay fallow, so it would be ready for the spring, now they had their own boat to ferry the horse across?

Daniel said, yes, without taking his eyes off Malin and Kaja, and added that it should be possible, maybe, and his father nodded.

They were put in the same luxurious room, with a view of the sea. But Ingrid couldn't sleep. Not a trace remained of all these weeks, not a single imprint, but she could see once more her father and mother and the North Chamber, so much so that it made her ears ring as she sat on the edge of the bed beside Kaja, who was asleep, and gazed across the water to Barrøy, a clear, blue silhouette against the horizon, it became even bluer and then turned completely black, before vanishing from her eyes.

EPILOGUE

The weather was clear and the sea was calm in late October 1946. Ingrid Marie Barrøy was washing up in the kitchen of the newly painted house and could follow the progress of the milk boat through the north-facing window – a slow-moving, white streak in the water until it disappeared and then reappeared in the west-facing window. She moved the soap swisher around in the lukewarm dishwater and was wondering whether to add some hot water when she noticed that the boat had changed course.

She dried her hands on her apron, grabbed a cardigan, went out onto the steps and saw that the vessel was heading for the new quay on a day when neither milk was to be collected, nor post delivered.

Down on the quay, Barbro was standing like a blue pillar, next to Kaja, who could walk now. Although Ingrid couldn't see from here, she knew her aunt wasn't holding her by the hand but firmly around her forearm, as always when they were by the sea. Ingrid checked that she didn't let go of Kaja when she made a grab for the hawser – and set off towards them.

There was a spring tide, the skipper opened the gate in the gunwale, and Mariann Vollheim lifted her coat and stepped ashore in one *long* stride, put down a green suitcase on the red granite church floor and knelt down in front of Kaja. Ingrid speeded up, but walked the final steps as if through glue and waited patiently until Mariann had risen to her feet again, a hand still resting on Kaja's head, and heard her say:

"How tall she's grown. I think she recognises me."

"A'm sure she does," Ingrid said.

Mariann's next words were directed across the island and to the sea:

"So this is yours?"

Ingrid realised that now *she* was the one in the know, and Mariann the one who had come begging.

She briefly greeted the skipper, a young man by the name of Johannes, closed the gate in the gunwale again, handed him the hawser, and asked Barbro to see to the suitcase and Kaja, then announced in an excessively formal tone – to her own ears – that she would show the guest around the island, they could follow the coast all the way, where there was no path, there were rocky shores. And Mariann said that would be nice.

Ingrid led her past the Swedes' boathouse and south over the solid rock, into which an iron peg had been hammered, and she made no comment. They walked past Love Grove, which from the house resembled an eyebrow on the crag, but at close range consisted of only four straggly birch trees that stood motionless in the calm air. Ingrid couldn't remember how it got its name, and didn't comment on them either.

She took a step to the left and waited until her guest had scrambled up beside her. Mariann was dressed in a burgundy coat, which was appropriate for autumn. She was also wearing slim, black-leather shoes with zips on the heels and lambskin gloves, and had curls that didn't suit her and lips that were too red, and on top of that she now wiped a lambskin finger under the tip of her nose to make sure it wasn't running.

Ingrid was well aware that Mariann hadn't dressed smartly for Barrøy or for her or Kaja, and when they stopped Mariann told her she was going back to teaching, at the prestigious Cathedral School in Trondheim, but had decided to make a trip north first, and visit Ingrid.

"He's not hier," Ingrid said.

"Are you trying to act stupid again?" Mariann snapped, suddenly turned and screamed hysterically at the sea, using words Ingrid didn't understand. She wanted to hold her back from the rock edge, but couldn't bring herself to catch hold of her, and then Mariann slumped down into the heather with a groan, and put her head in her gloved hands.

Ingrid sat down beside her, and they remained there until Mariann apologised and asked Ingrid if she had found out anything.

Ingrid said Mariann should tell *her* what *she* knew.

Mariann asked if she was trying to punish her. Ingrid said, no. Mariann said that if she was, she had every right to do so, but she wasn't used to this kind of treatment.

Ingrid said she wasn't giving her any kind of treatment.

"Are you trying to be funny?"

"No," Ingrid said.

They gazed at the skerries. Mariann said that if they had met before she lost her children, Ingrid would understand her situation, she was a completely different woman then. Ingrid said she had no way of knowing.

"Say something then," Mariann said.

"Hva does tha want me t' say?" Ingrid said.

"For God's sake," Mariann sniffled. And they sat stock-still through Ingrid's silence until Mariann gave up and suggested carrying on.

Mariann walked on the barely visible path, and Ingrid on the heather. Ingrid led the way across the rocks along the coast like a bellwether, turned and took Mariann by the hand and helped her up a steep crag letting go of it again as soon as they were on top and had a view over the small islands on the horizon, which offered Barrøy the meagre protection it needed to avoid total disaster.

They continued down to the beach and sat on the marble-white tree trunk that not even Our Lord was able to budge. Ingrid told her that they had found it after it had been washed ashore some time in her childhood and they had sawn off its arms and legs. And Mariann placed her hands on it as if to test whether it lived up to its promise, and asked Ingrid if she wasn't cold, only wearing a cardigan.

"No," Ingrid said. "An' tha?"

Mariann didn't answer. And they continued to sit stock-still, until Mariann took a deep breath and said that now Ingrid had left her with no choice. She unbuttoned her coat and took out a folded letter and handed it to her. Ingrid was taken aback, opened it and recognised what she saw, the nine identical lines she couldn't read, but could understand, Alexander's declaration of love, for *her*.

"This is mine," she said starchily, looking down at the paper.

"No," Mariann said. "It's mine."

"Hvur did tha get tha hands on this?"

"He gave it to me before they set out across the ice."

Ingrid said she didn't believe that for a minute.

Mariann said she could believe whatever she wanted.

Ingrid stared at the Cyrillic letters and counted the lines, and knew that this put them in the same boat, and the little that her journey had not been able to destroy had now been destroyed nonetheless, she was the same as Mariann.

The cat came around the tree trunk and jumped up into her lap. Ingrid began to scratch it behind the ear. They heard laughter and shouting from the Karvika kids, who were playing by the old wheelhouse in Bosom Acre. Ingrid turned and managed to recite their names, noticing that her voice held and that

264

Mariann seemed to be listening. Then she also noticed that up by the buildings Barbro and Suzanne were outside in the bright weather, dressed as though they were indoors – she couldn't see from here, but knew that Suzanne had Kaja in her arms, and that decided the matter.

Mariann eyed her.

Ingrid put down the cat, gave Mariann the letter back and looked out to sea as she told her how Alexander and Henrik had made it alive through the mountains that winter from Høgmo, about their journey to Brynet, made special mention of their stay at the hotel in Trondheim, the clean beds and the hot water, and concluded by telling her how Alexander had been repatri-ated eighteen months ago, from Sonderlager Mysen. She also told her about Maria in Leningrad and their by now five-year-old son, who had been named after his father.

But she didn't mention anything about how he had damaged his hands, she didn't have the heart. And Mariann looked as though this was exactly what she had come all this way to hear, or had hoped to hear, even though she said she didn't believe a word of it, it was too good to be true.

Ingrid said she could believe whatever she wanted, it was get-ting cold now, they should go up to the house and light the fire in the parlour, then she would show her some photographs.

There was something else on her mind, where to put her guest. But they had got no further than the middle of Rose Acre when she decided she had no option but to accept Mariann would have to be with her and Kaja in the North Chamber, there was no other room in the house. And Mariann said that if she was planning to show her photos of Alexander, then she didn't want to see them. Ingrid said she had to.

Mariann didn't answer.

But she took off her coat and also her gloves, to help Ingrid with the stove. Then she removed her shoes and was given a pair of lugg boots to wear, and when the room had warmed up and Ingrid had got out the photographs, they sat with their backs to the south-facing window, allowing the light to stream in between them.

Alexander Mihailovich Nizhnikov, together with just under four hundred other Russian prisoners-of-war, was marched out of Sonderlager Mysen on June 18, 1945, and made to board a train which in the course of four and a half days transported them through Sweden and Finland, whereafter they were taken by bus to a camp on the outskirts of a town named Kem in Russian Karelia.

Here, they were informed that in accordance with Stalin's Decree No. 270 of August 16, 1941 they were not to be regarded as liberated prisoners-of-war but as traitors.

Alexander and three of his friends from Mysen were subjected to a summary interrogation, and the accounts of all four were categorised as unreliable, unprovable, unlikely. They were fed, allowed to take a bath, dressed in prison uniforms and put on another train, which in the course of thirteen days transported them to a gulag camp eighty kilometres south of Khabarovsk in Eastern Siberia, where all trace of the four men ends.

BIBLIOASIS INTERNATIONAL TRANSLATION SERIES
General Editor: Stephen Henighan

1. *I Wrote Stone: The Selected Poetry of*
Ryszard Kapuściński (Poland)
Translated by Diana Kuprel & Marek Kusiba

2. *Good Morning Comrades*
by Ondjaki (Angola)
Translated by Stephen Henighan

3. *Kahn & Engelmann*
by Hans Eichner (Austria-Canada)
Translated by Jean M. Snook

4. *Dance With Snakes*
by Horacio Castellanos Moya (El Salvador)
Translated by Lee Paula Springer

5. *Black Alley*
by Mauricio Segura (Quebec)
Translated by Dawn M. Cornelio

6. *The Accident*
by Mihail Sebastian (Romania)
Translated by Stephen Henighan

7. *Love Poems*
by Jaime Sabines (Mexico)
Translated by Colin Carberry

8. *The End of the Story*
by Liliana Heker (Argentina)
Translated by Andrea G. Labinger

9. *The Tuner of Silences*
by Mia Couto (Mozambique)
Translated by David Brookshaw

10. *For as Far as the Eye Can See*
by Robert Melançon (Quebec)
Translated by Judith Cowan

11. *Eucalyptus*
by Mauricio Segura (Quebec)
Translated by Donald Winkler

12. *Granma Nineteen and the Soviet's Secret*
by Ondjaki (Angola)
Translated by Stephen Henighan

13. *Montreal Before Spring*
by Robert Melançon (Quebec)
Translated by Donald McGrath

14. *Pensativities: Essays and Provocations*
by Mia Couto (Mozambique)
Translated by David Brookshaw

15. *Arvida*
by Samuel Archibald (Quebec)
Translated by Donald Winkler

16. *The Orange Grove*
by Larry Tremblay (Quebec)
Translated by Sheila Fischman

17. *The Party Wall*
by Catherine Leroux (Quebec)
Translated by Lazer Lederhendler

18. *Black Bread*
by Emili Teixidor (Catalonia)
Translated by Peter Bush

19. *Boundary*
by Andrée A. Michaud (Quebec)
Translated by Donald Winkler

20. *Red, Yellow, Green*
by Alejandro Saravia (Bolivia-Canada)
Translated by María José Giménez